MW01608528

# Praise for Portia Da Costa's
## *Far From Perfect*

"...characters worth caring about and a nice swoony ending."

~ *Basia's Bookshelf*

Look for these titles by
*Portia Da Costa*

*Now Available:*

A Touch of Heaven

# Far From Perfect

*Portia Da Costa*

Samhain Publishing, Ltd.
11821 Mason Montgomery Road, 4B
Cincinnati, OH 45249
www.samhainpublishing.com

Far From Perfect
Copyright © 2012 by Portia Da Costa
Print ISBN: 978-1-60928-409-1
Digital ISBN: 978-1-60928-269-1

Editing by Heidi Moore
Cover by Kendra Egert

This book is a work of fiction. The names, characters, places, and incidents are products of the writer's imagination or have been used fictitiously and are not to be construed as real. Any resemblance to persons, living or dead, actual events, locale or organizations is entirely coincidental.

All Rights Are Reserved. No part of this book may be used or reproduced in any manner whatsoever without written permission, except in the case of brief quotations embodied in critical articles and reviews.

First Samhain Publishing, Ltd. electronic publication: March 2011
First Samhain Publishing, Ltd. print publication: January 2012

# Prologue

It was now or never. She'd waited too many years already, yearning like a half-baked damsel in distress, hoping he'd see her the way she saw him. If she held back much longer she might never get a chance.

Anna Felgate padded forward into the darkened bedroom, guided by a shaft of moonlight that spilt onto the bed from the open window...and illuminated an angel.

Niccolo Lisitano, the son of her father's dearest friend. Niccolo Lisitano, the man she'd loved since she was barely more than a girl.

He stirred slightly as she approached, but he was still dead to the world, sleeping the sleep of the weary traveler who was mired in jet lag but happy to be home. It probably wasn't the best time to wake him up and offer herself to him like sex on a plate, but she was sick to death of being a virgin, and spending another holiday wanting but not having.

The scents of summer roses, citrus and balsam oozed into the room from the groves above the villa, and the night was warm and heavy-aired, like velvet on her skin as she stripped off her vest and sleep shorts. Nick was naked too, and feeling the heat just as she did, judging by the way he'd thrown aside the single sheet on his bed. He was facing away from her, exhibiting his perfect profile and the shine of tanned skin over taut, sculpted musculature. Shoulders, back, thighs and buttocks, all perfect to her eyes. His golden hair gleamed against the white of the pillow, darker in the shadows than in the sun, but still glorious.

Settling herself gingerly, she climbed onto the bed. But despite her care, Nick sensed her weight, turned slowly and began to shake his way to wakefulness. He groaned, rubbed his face and pushed his hand through his tousled curls. Even sleepy and grimacing, he was everything Anna wanted, and she gasped, sideswiped anew as her heart clenched in longing. The perfumed air and the beauty of the man before her were a drug that made her feel as if she were dreaming too. In that dream she was a goddess who could do anything, even when Nick's eyes snapped open, and recognition dawned in their blue depths.

"Anna?" He blinked, still hazy and fighting towards full consciousness. As if on autopilot, he reached out blindly, trying to find the sheet and cover himself, but Anna wasn't having of that. She'd waited too long to see all of him, every last gorgeous inch, especially the penis that she'd driven herself half-mad speculating about when she'd watched him poolside in form-fitting Speedos. Before he could get a grip on the bedlinen, she set her knee on it so he couldn't pull it up.

Still frowning, Nick came up on one elbow, peering at her in the low light, his brows shooting up when he registered her bare body. Triumph buoyed her up when she saw the flare in his eyes, the heat he couldn't hide, and the way his unsuppressed gaze traveled over her, licking her skin like a flame. At last he was seeing her, really seeing her.

"What are you doing here, *cara*?"

But there was still confusion in his eyes, and his voice was blurred with sleep. She could feel the war going on in him. The conflict between status quo and the ancient male urge already making his sex rise. "Look, you shouldn't—"

*No! You're not sending me away. I won't let you.*

She didn't say it. She wasn't going to plead like a little girl shrilling for a piece of candy. She was twenty, and a woman, even if she was a virgin. So instead she just reached out and placed her fingers across his lips, then an instant later she replaced her fingers with her mouth.

At first, he seemed to resist her, as if his subconscious was clinging to the idea of her as his familiar "holiday buddy".

*No way, mister,* she thought, banishing her doubts as she sought to crush his by pressing forward and kissing him as if her life depended on it.

His mouth was like velvet, firm and supple, deliciously warm. As she ran her tongue along the inner edges of his lips, they parted, letting her in. He was quiescent, but only for a moment, and then his tongue pressed against hers, making it yield, asserting his dominance.

*Yes, yes, yes!*

Instead of holding back now, he surged forward, brushing her hair away from her face as he compelled her back against the pillow. Anna rearranged herself to fit him, stretching her body down the bed, molding as much of her skin against as much of his as she could. She gasped into his mouth when his penis brushed her thigh, then pressed harder against it.

He was solid, hot, growing, the skin like satin. Anna's prime instinct was to rub herself against him, and she followed it, loving the way he growled low in his throat even while he was still kissing her. She curled her arms around him, running her fingers over his backside and his thighs, still rubbing, still circling her sex against him as he worked his sex against her.

He felt perfect. He wanted her. The night and the man were

the embodiment of her dreams.

The kiss deepened. His hands roved her body, cupping her breasts, skimming over her bottom. He was possessive and hungry, but at the same time gentle and measured. Even as she simmered and trembled at his touch, she wondered. Did he suspect he was the first? He drew back and peered into her eyes in the darkness, his own questioning. Her answer was a smile, and a sultry kiss against his neck. She drew confidence from his beauty and his scent and the strength of his erection.

Unable to stop herself, she reached down between their bodies to caress him.

"Oh, Anna...yes, yes," he murmured, surging in her hold. She'd never done this before, but the way he moved and gasped and arched his neck all told her that she was doing something right, even though she was far from the experienced kind of woman he was used to. A man like Nick knew how to keep himself in check, but still, she stroked him only lightly, handling his penis with reverence. His low, thrilling moans only confirmed her instinct to go lightly.

After a few moments, he shook his head against the pillow, and she froze.

"Enough," he gasped, his voice as shadowy as the night. "My turn to touch—" he stilled her hand and put it from him, "—and yours to be touched." He looked down at her, and for a moment he frowned, his eyes cloudy again, as if he still wasn't quite sure he was awake. Then he settled his lips on hers and slid his palm down the length of her body, curving over waist and hips and thighs. As he pushed his tongue into her mouth again, he dipped his fingers between her thighs.

The sensation was electric, wonderful, just as she'd imagined it, but more, different, better. Ready, willing and tense with long-brewed desire, she was halfway to the pinnacle already. Moaning and moving, she pushed against him, rising and rocking as he stroked her and kissed her face and throat.

Within moments, she climaxed hard, shouting his name, stunned and stopped in her tracks by the intensity of it. The sensations were unreal and yet everything she'd imagined and hoped for and more.

But sweet as the pleasure was, after a few moments of pause she was eager to taste it again, and ready to give as well as take.

Embracing, kissing, touching and sliding their bodies against each other, the hunger and passion rose and swelled like gathering waves, each one gaining momentum. For a long time, they enjoyed each other, playing and exploring, mostly silent apart from gasps and whispers and moans, most barely coherent. They didn't join, but did almost every other wonderful thing that Anna had practiced in her imagination with the dream of Nick.

Then the time came.

Nick's eyes were intent, serious, yet fiery in the darkness, still asking questions. Anna simply kissed him and pushed herself against him, impatient even while he rolled on a condom. Her heart quivered and she could hardly breathe with excitement when he moved between her thighs. And pressed into her, sighing her name.

It hurt a little and she caught her breath.

Nick halted, mid-thrust, and tried to make her look in his eyes. But she buried her head against his neck, and arched her body against him, determined to take him into her by sheer force of will.

"Anna? Are you all right? What is it?" His voice was tight, fierce, on the ragged edge of self-control. Anna felt him trying to pull back, but she clung on hard, redoubling her efforts.

"I'm fine...great...wonderful..." she gasped again, "I was just a little tense...I'm so excited...Nick, please...I want you in me."

There was an instant, just an instant, when she sensed him disbelieving her, and still inclined to retreat. So she stroked his back and his bottom and thighs, her fingers traveling and teasing, making him groan and renew his efforts.

Then it was easy. At last. And Nick loved her in a rhythm that was deep and sweet and true, and she matched him, rising and meeting him, stroke for stroke, riding the groundswell of their pleasure, the passion and desire, until at last they soared together to the precious peak of orgasm.

As they lay afterwards, waiting for their breath and for the world around them to normalize, Anna shuddered. It was almost as if one moment she was in heaven, the next in another place entirely. She couldn't describe it or pinpoint why, but as the silence between them lengthened and lengthened, a strange cold breeze wafted in from the garden, more North Sea than the balmy Mediterranean.

She stared at Nick in the darkness beside her and her stomach dropped in alarm. His body was a column of tension, and his face was a chiaroscuro of complex emotions, his beauty hard and unforgiving. Expressions shifted and changed across his features even as she watched, cycling through anger, regret, self-loathing and others less definable. Then he frowned and suddenly spoke, his voice hard and tight as he reached for the sheet and draped it across her.

"You young idiot, you were a virgin, weren't you?"

The northern waters deluged all over Anna's head, dowsing away the drowsy heat of passion and chilling the warmth of love. She couldn't speak.

"How could you be so stupid?" Nick's tone was as stern and cool as his face, and after a moment of frigid shock, a new kind of heat surged in Anna's gut.

*How dare you? How dare you go all sanctimonious and disapproving on me in the blink of an eye after what we just did?*

Not so long ago, he'd been enjoying everything she had to offer, but now it was as if she was in bed with a different man entirely. Not the lovable, funny, companionable Nick she'd always known, and not the generous, searing, magnificent lover of just a few minutes ago.

No, this was a new man, as dead and distant the moon and yet strangely aggressive. A million miles away, yet beside her. A new rush of horror dawned. Oh God, was this the real Nick, the one she'd never seen, the predatory self-serving egotist? Was she just another woman to be savored for the briefest while, then discarded?

*Don't be stupid. That's what you wanted him for, wasn't it? To rid you of your virginity, no strings, no entanglement?*

But still, still she knew she'd wanted more, much more, fool that she was. Anger with herself as well as him made her aggressive too.

"Yes, of course I was a virgin, Nick. What's the problem in that? Every woman is until her first time. It's not unusual." Her voice rang out in the quiet room, far more strident and pugnacious than she wanted it to be. She hadn't really worked out in advance how she'd deal with the aftermath, but all shreds of good sense and reason had been dissolved by Nick's sudden hostility. "I thought you'd be pleased. I thought men like you liked deflowering virgins?"

"Men like me? Players, you mean? Men who get through a lot of women?" He was storming now too, his dark eyes sparkling with anger. Although a still, quiet voice in Anna's mind observed that he was probably as furious with himself as she was with herself.

13

Shaking his head, Nick reached for his robe, pulled it on and cinched it tight, then turned and glared at her, "*Per Dio,* what on earth were you thinking, Anna?"

*Clearly I wasn't thinking at all,* thought Anna later, feeling as if she'd been pounded by rocks as she mentally replayed the ebb and flow of the rest of their argument. She'd cringed at their stiff, tight-lipped agreement in the aftermath.

They would never speak of tonight. It hadn't happened, and it was better that way. Better for them. Better for the family.

But still her heart turned over with sorrow at the thought of what *had* happened. And what they'd lost. Most probably forever.

How could something that started so perfectly grow so far from it?

# Chapter One

*Four Years Later.*

Niccolo Lisitano stood beneath a tree in a small London square, staring at the lighted windows of the tall Regency house across the road. It was drizzling, and the moisture was gathering on his skin and making his hair curl, but he still felt reluctant to cross the road and knock for entrance.

Nick wasn't a craven or cautious man. In fact his self-confidence was usually rock-solid, a suit of armor with few if any cracks. But the hours ahead could be awkward and emotionally messy if he didn't pitch things exactly right. It was a delicate plan, and a gamble, and he still hadn't quite completely thought it through, which was rare for him. But he'd never shied away from gambles in his life, and he wasn't about to turn his back on this one.

Still he hesitated, monitoring the rectangles of yellow radiance and the shadows of partygoers moving in elegant rooms. Was she there? Of course she was there. It was her father's birthday. The father she loved and would do anything for, just as he would do anything for his. Hence his mission tonight.

Reaching beneath his dark overcoat and into the pocket of his suit, Nick drew out a folded page from a celebrity magazine and opened it up to show the image he'd found himself studying disturbingly often since he'd acquired it a few days ago. It had the same effect on him that it'd had the first time he'd looked at it.

*It's just a picture, fool. Don't lose control. She's beautiful and you care about her, but she's not going to be easy to persuade, no matter how hard you try and how much you still want her, even now.*

But still his heart thumped and his groin tightened.

*Anna Felgate and friend*, the caption read. Ignoring the man whose hand she was holding and the laughing group of people around them, his eyes lingered over the image of the slim bright-eyed blonde woman in a sexy little vintage party dress. She was beautiful, more now than ever. But then she'd always been stunning, even when she'd been just a girl and their relationship had been innocent, just buddies.

Anna Felgate was the daughter of one of his father's oldest friends, and she'd always been feisty and undaunted by life. Ever his cherished companion and rival during holidays in both England and Italy, Anna had never been afraid to speak her mind and challenge him, despite their twelve-year age gap. She'd always reached out boldly for what she wanted.

Then one night, she'd been more than bold. One night she'd been exquisite and crazy and made him act in a way that was even crazier.

His long fingers clenched involuntarily, almost crushing the precious tear-out. He no longer saw Anna's bright smile for the paparazzi, nor her pretty elfin haircut, nor her quirky individualistic outfit that suited her so sweetly. Instead, those astonishing green eyes gazed up at him from the deep shadows of a Mediterranean night, brilliant as jewels with anticipation and excitement, pupils black and dilated with desire. Her long, pale hair fanned out across his pillow, framing her face and her bare, satiny shoulders. Along the full length of his body he could feel her daringly naked, all warmth and irresistible female perfection, his for the taking.

Drawing in a deep, ragged breath, Nick smoothed out the increasingly water-splashed picture as best he could, remembering the thrill of running his fingertips over her body. She'd been more rounded in the darkness of his bed than she was now, the years had refined her and made her sleek and toned. But she was still that perfect vision of delicious, entrancing womanhood, and the stirring of his body only confirmed how much she moved him. He was hard now, painfully so, the sensation impossible to ignore or suppress. It was a battle he'd fought whenever they'd met since that one single night of passion in Italy.

*Dannazione!* As if the evening ahead wasn't fraught with enough complications as it was. He half wished for the heavens to really open, and drench him to the bone, to douse his fires.

Looking up to the night sky, Nick dragged in air, his chest expanding like an athlete's as he composed his mind for the showdown ahead. He would achieve nothing if he lost his cool, and closing his eyes, he gave thanks for what rain there was as it pattered onto his face, soft and calming. After moment or two, he was able to look down again at the damp sheet of torn-out paper, and frowned at the fact Anna was with a man.

*If I don't act now, I'm in trouble. She'll settle for the latest of these bland, inoffensive nonentities she seems to go for, and that'll mean the end of my plans, no matter how half-formed they are.*

Taking a deep breath, he folded the page again, wryly aware that he was taking the utmost care not to place a crease across Anna's face. Then, as he slipped it back into his pocket, he squared his shoulders with purpose and strode out across

17

the square towards the Felgate house and the party.

Not into battle as such, though a part of him expected it.


On hearing the front doorbell, Anna Felgate shuddered with a sudden, crawling sense of premonition.

"Will you answer it, sweetheart?" her father asked, his eyes brightening. She knew he'd been putting a brave face on things for her sake, given all the financial uncertainty. The economic downturn had hit his manufacturing business hard, and she knew he'd been faced with some worrying numbers, but all of a sudden he looked genuinely excited and optimistic. "I just want to check something with the caterer."

A scan of the room revealed everything going smoothly, and drinks and nibbles circulating efficiently, but Anna shrugged. If Dad wanted to check on the catering that was his prerogative. It was his birthday. So, with a quick smile, she sped towards the front door to let in the tardy guest. She knew her late mother would have made a far more efficient hostess than she did, and it was at times like these she missed her more than usual, and longed for the sense of welcome and being cherished.

*Maybe it's Martin?* she thought, trying to squash a mild sense of unease. He'd said he'd try and get here if he could, but a craven part of her rather wished he wouldn't make it. She was going to have to do *something* about herself and Martin, and do it quickly. It wasn't fair to him, and she hated feeling like a fraud.

The doorbell chimed again, this time long and impatiently. "Oh, keep your hair on," she muttered. Bloody hell, if it was Martin he was being a damn sight more assertive than usual. The way he was abusing the bell reminded her much more of a certain other person. A person her father would be much happier for her to pair up with, on a permanent basis if possible.

*No, no, no! That book is closed, idiot. Locked and bound with chains and consigned to the bottom of the ocean.*

And yet, even as she tried to squelch the fantasies that even after all these years would not be squelched, her steps faltered and her heart drummed guiltily beneath the silk embroidery on her bodice.

It was too late. She'd done it now. It *could* be him, even though to her knowledge there'd been no formal answer to the invitation they'd sent him. And the mega-jitters, the shallow breathing and the maniacal thumping of her blood were her natural response, even though there was still a chance it might be Martin who never provoked any of those reactions.

But the door swung open with a fatalistic inevitability, revealing the person her heart and gut had known would be there. Anna's smile froze, her jaw tightened and the bright, half-prepared words of greeting expired on her lips. For just a millisecond, she was bereft of the power of speech altogether, but then self-possession kicked back in and she mustered her voice.

"Nick! Hello. How lovely to see you. I'm so glad you were able to make it."

Amazing. Such eloquence. Was that all she could manage? Apparently, yes, because Niccolo Lisitano's ability to take her breath away was still fully intact, and now he seemed to have stolen her command of the Queen's English too.

"Good evening, Anna."

The lean, dark-clad figure on the doorstep smiled. His oh-so-familiar devastating grin looked so real, so genuine, despite everything. Maybe it was? "Can I come in then?"

What if she *didn't* invite him in? Could she just shut the

19

door and leave him and his animal magnetism or whatever it was out there? For a moment, she entertained notions about vampires and demons that couldn't come in if you didn't invite them, then dashed them away, telling herself not to be mad.

"Yes...yes, of course. Come in." Anna stepped quickly back. Almost too quickly. Her body reacted to something the eye couldn't see, and that shouldn't really exist. A kind of *field* of dazzling energy that always seemed to surround Nick. It had been almost a year since she'd last seen him, but the effect was always the same. "You're always welcome here," she added, attempting to project casual friendliness, even though she had a nasty feeling she wasn't succeeding—and that Nick knew it.

"Of course." He was already just inches from her, moving faster than seemed natural, and already far too close for her peace of mind.

The voice was as ever deep and soft, playful yet utterly assured. Against her will, Anna's eyes devoured the strong, athletic frame, enhanced rather than hidden by his perfectly tailored suit and the long black overcoat he wore open despite the spring drizzle outside. His tawny-gold, sun-bleached hair was bedewed with rain and there was a light sheen of moisture across his familiar and almost unfairly handsome features.

Time had passed, and a stray line or two had appeared around his eyes, yet still that near-perfect male face seemed to have been in her mind constantly. She stared into his blue gaze and found it cool and assessing, and infinitely disturbing.

Yet was there a shadow there, a flicker of acknowledgement of all they'd agreed to bury? Or was it a question? She remembered a time—the long hazy summers of her girlhood—when those amazing eyes had sparkled only with warmth and a rascally older-brother affection towards her. And there was a time just once when they'd been velvet dark with passion.

"What a filthy night." Banishing that thought with another bright smile, she attempted to breathe as normally and unobtrusively as possible whilst feeling as if she'd just run a marathon. But she couldn't hide anything from Nick. His laser gaze zeroed in instantaneously on the lift and fall of her breasts beneath her delicate silk and lace top.

"Don't worry. I enjoy the rain." His eyes flicked back to her face only after a long, assessing pause, "It's refreshing. It clarifies the thoughts."

*Clarifies them for what?*

Anna's stomach swooped. What was going on in that devious razor of a mind? And why had he suddenly looked at her in *that* way, the way they'd agreed did not, had never existed between them? She searched his face for clues, but it was unreadable again. Stunning, as perfectly carved as ever, but now completely opaque to her.

"Yes...right." She felt herself starting to flounder. How could he send her into a flat spin in just a few seconds and with a few innocuous words?

"Did you have a good flight? Where are you staying? When did you arrive?"

She flung questions at him, not really seeking answers, but just for something, anything, to say.

His eyes narrowed and she knew she'd made a mistake. Or at least she thought she had. A moment later, amusement softened the harder lines of his face and his mouth, always his most sensuous, almost voluptuous feature, curved in a way that made her heart skip and gallop and her knees turn to paper.

"Is this an interrogation?"

Staring down at her, he laced his fingers in front of him, lights dancing in those marvelous, magical eyes.

"No! Of course not. I'm just making small talk." The words were quick and flustered, and emotion rioted inside, making her rash. "As we always do."

His dark blond brows lifted, and if a man as composed as Nick could be said to flinch, he appeared to. He mimed the word, *touché* then went on smoothly as if the small moment of conflict and real communication as opposed to play-acting had never existed. "Well then, I arrived around two, and I'm staying at the Savoy. And I didn't fly. I drove from Italy."

That stood to reason. *Industria Lisitano* was a huge conglomerate with diverse holdings, but the automotive division, especially the high-performance sports cars, had always been Nick's baby. And he never missed a chance to get behind the wheel of their latest offering.

"That's some drive." Hyper-awareness of him created the image of the interior of a supercar, cramped and intimate, herself beside him, and only inches between their bodies, their thighs. The relative spaciousness of the hall seemed to close in on them. "May I take your coat," she added quickly, reaching out.

*This is the first time we've actually been completely alone together since...*

It dawned on her like a thunderbolt, and her hands stilled and dropped to her sides.

*No! We don't go there.*

But it was too late. The interior of some fast car or other morphed into that of a darkened bedroom, an envelope of Mediterranean heat, with the scents of pine and lemon groves and aroused man flooding her senses.

"Is something wrong?"

The question sounded genuine and concerned, yet the low, almost purring note in his voice played across her strung-out nerves.

"No... Nothing at all," she claimed, feigning a calm, untroubled cheerfulness she didn't feel.

*Yes! Everything,* an inner, disorientated voice cried. *Please go back to Italy, Nick, and don't make things complicated.* Flashing him a twinkling smile to match his own, she finally reached for his coat.

Nick's face was a picture. His smile was the most amazing she'd ever seen, yet somehow she could feel a frown in there too, and complex feelings playing out behind his mask of glamour. Automatically, she worried for him, as she always did, despite everything. Then the darkness was gone again, and for half a second she got the distinct impression that he intended to turn around, stretch out his arms and let her relieve him of the coat like some kind of dutiful parlor maid. But instead he shrugged elegantly out of the long, dark garment himself and caught it behind him before shaking it free of raindrops and handing it to her.

Hanging the coat up gave Anna a moment breathing space when she wasn't forced to look directly into Nick's face and be subject to that bamboozled, sideswiped feeling he induced in her. She had to think straight, and as she did a wash of guilt gripped her. Dear God, she hadn't even asked about Carlo.

"How is your father doing? Is he feeling better?" As she turned back towards him she caught the pain crossing his face, and her heart turned over in sympathy. The relationship between Italian sons and their fathers was often turbulent, and particularly so in Nick and Carlo's case, but filial love ran far deeper than antipathy.

"He's doing well... Being a pain in the hindquarters, as usual, so yes, definitely improved."

Nick seemed very still somehow. It was a quality he

sometimes possessed, and in the narrow confines of the hall it was amplified and bizarrely felt almost energetic. The impact of his body just inches away from hers buffeted Anna's senses and sent flight-or-fight instinct racing through her. But she stomped it down ruthlessly and focused on more tangible matters. "Uncle" Carlo had always been extravagantly kind to her and news of his heart attack and major surgery had been a horrible shock. She'd wanted to visit, despite the fact she'd almost certainly run into Nick, but the medics had insisted on quiet and only the very immediate family as visitors.

"He was most insistent on me coming here to represent him," Nick went on with a wry smile that made Anna's stomach flutter. "Especially with Sofia too heavily pregnant to leave Rome," he added, referring to his happily married sister, "And Pietro, naturally, wanting to stay close to her."

"Of course. And are they well too?" she enquired.

Pleasantries, polite social niceties, family chit-chat. Was this what they were eternally reduced to? She felt awkward and somehow despairing as Nick nodded in reply.

"Look, come on through, Dad will be thrilled to see you."

"So you're playing quite the little hostess tonight, eh?" observed Nick, still not moving, his blue, unblinking eyes pinning her to the tiled floor.

"I *am* the hostess, and I'm not little."

The words were out of her lips almost before she'd thought them and she could have kicked herself for losing it with him so quickly.

"I'm sorry. I didn't mean that to sound derogatory. I was just making small talk and it came out wrong."

The apology rang true as a bell, and she knew it was honestly tendered, but at the same time there was an infinite fieriness in Nick's blue eyes, a quality both combative and

24

intoxicating. Their four years of cordial, manufactured smiles and unspoken distance keeping suddenly fell away like a sheet of shattered glass. "I cannot think of anyone other than you that I'd prefer to welcome me to this party," he added softly.

*What are you up to? We agreed "that night" never happened. So there's no need for us to dance around each other like cats spoiling for a fight.*

"Sorry," she backtracked, "I'm a bit nervous about everything going right tonight, that's all." She gestured towards the open door of the reception room beyond and the sound of laughing voices and conversation. The sound of sanctuary. "Please, come on...Dad will be wondering where I've got to and who's arrived."

But as she took a step, Nick caught her by the arm, his hand like a gauntlet of fire gripping her bare skin. Sensation rocketed through her, activating...everything. Another first in all the truce years. Long suppressed physical responses switched instantaneously into high gear. Only an effort of pure will stopped her wrenching herself away from him.

Either that or throwing herself forward into his arms.

*"Tra un momento."*

Nick's usually accentless voice sounded all Latin, and the fact he'd lapsed momentarily into his native tongue was disquieting. "There's something I need to discuss with you." His fingers tightened on her arm, the very subtlety of the hold more disquieting than any amount of force or coercion. "In private. In the library?" He nodded towards the door that led to Clive's cozy book-filled sanctum, the hall light glinting on his gilded hair with the slight motion. He might be all dark Italian fire inside, but he'd inherited the full effect of his English mother's blonde beauty. His looks were the very embodiment of the head-on clash of passion and emotion between his parents. He was a mythical beast forged in a caldron of joy and pain.

"Right now?" she enquired, dragging herself back from past Lisitano dramas to the present one that faced her.

"Right now."

The core of steel in the two words made her blood run cold, and then very, very hot.

Without further protest, she allowed herself to be led.

"I'll get straight down to business," Nick announced the moment they were in the room, closing the door with an ominous click. Like an imperious potentate, he bade her sit, then strode across the room, lithe and purposeful.

In front of a tall bookcase he turned swiftly, the fluid tailoring of his jacket causing the light fabric to flare and reveal his body beneath. He looked fit and powerful, maybe leaner than when she'd last seen him, and the dark clothing he so often wore only highlighted his relentless yet elegant sexuality.

*Get a grip, Anna! Don't let him turn you into a giant, idiotic hormone with his gorgeousness. He* knows *he's doing it.*

And yet her body seemed to sizzle as if he'd flung her on a griddle. "I wish you would," she said, keeping her voice level and pleasant. Even managing a *faux* relaxed smile.

"I have a proposition for you, Anna." He fixed her with a scrutiny so intense the world faded away around them. "I want your help, if you're prepared to give it. In fact, I need it."

For a moment he hesitated, which was so unlike him, flipping back the panels of his suit jacket and thrusting his hands into his pockets. The action showcased his narrow hips and the general area of his groin in a way that made Anna blink and go light-headed.

"I'm listening." Her cleverly constructed calmness was rocking on the inside, but externally she almost sounded normal.

"Good. That's what I want. That you should listen to everything I have to say, absorb it carefully, and not interrupt."

"And then you'll take questions from the floor afterwards?"

Nick merely quirked his brow at her but Anna could see the Italian macho male in him shaking his head. He would never act impatient or throw his weight about, but he had a million subtle, barely detectable ways of showing displeasure.

"Right, sorry, I am listening," she shot back, offering another tight smile. He infuriated her, and he always had done—even if mostly in a playful way up until four years ago—but there was nothing to be gained by picking fights.

"As you know, my father's ill. He's undergone major surgery and has a hill of recovery to climb."

The tell-tails of strain passed across Nick's face again, and despite their differences and barriers and complications, Anna wanted to hold him and offer comfort, offer solace. He must be in an agony of worry over Carlo. She couldn't begin to imagine how she'd feel if the same thing had happened to her father.

"He's out of critical danger now and he's making progress. But not as fast as the doctors—and I—really want him to. And sometimes, it almost seems he's not trying." Nick started to pace back and forth in front of the bookcase, which shocked Anna, given his special, predatory stillness. "I think he needs something to fix his hopes on. Something to cherish and look forward to."

Nick halted in his perambulations and suddenly turned towards Anna, "Goals have always worked for him in the past and they will again." Without warning, he threw himself down on the leather chesterfield beside her, the impact almost catapulting her towards him. As it was, the gap between them was just a perilous inch or two. "I've done all I can on the

27

business front. Not even the fact that we're still thriving and growing in such a tough economic climate can excite him."

Anna pictured Nick presenting examples of his phenomenal business acumen like gifts in an attempt to cheer Carlo up. He wouldn't show anxiety. Like most men of his culture, the elder Lisitano valued strength above all qualities in Italian manhood, and as he'd exhibited only moments ago, Nick could wear the world's most unrevealing poker face when it suited him. But that anxiety would be there because of the love the two men shared.

"No, it has to be something personal...something *family*, if you will, to really lift him."

Was Nick closer than ever now? He hadn't moved again since he'd flung himself down, but his proximity was like pressure all over her skin, and his unique cologne—fresh, yet exotic and spicy—was filtering into her brain and acting on both pleasure centers and areas of higher judgment.

"But surely he's thrilled about Sofia's baby?" Alarm and wild messages shot up and down a million nerve pathways, urging Anna to incline towards him until she tumbled into his arms. The gap was narrowing and the temptation to touch him made the tips of her fingers itch and prickle.

"Naturally, he is." Nick seemed unaware of the madness he was inciting, but then again, it was often hard to tell what was going on with him. "But Sofi has always been a good girl, a dutiful daughter in every way. The prospect of a grandchild delights Carlo, of course, but it's just what he's always expected of her."

Leaning back in the upholstered seat, Nick glanced away for a moment, looking down, then smoothing an imaginary wrinkle from the tailored perfection of his trouser knee. Momentarily unobserved, Anna bit her lip. His profile was hard and male, classic yet almost angelic, and the lushness and length of his surprisingly dark lashes veiled his eyes.

Nick's sudden sigh was strangely heartfelt. "No, nothing short of a grand gesture from *me* will give him the boost he needs." He looked up again and gave her a slanted, almost testing glance that invited her to second-guess the nature of that gesture.

Anna gasped. In the space of one thud of her racing heart, the weight of slight clues and long-cherished expectations reached critical mass.

*Oh no! Not that. He couldn't expect something like that, surely?*

Another clue dripped as he reached for her hand and enclosed her fingers in his, calm and cool and strong. After a four-year drought of touch between them, the impact was monumental, almost heart-stopping.

Almost as much as what she suspected was coming.

"I think you know what I want, don't you?" His eyes, like twin blue stars, were hypnotic. She couldn't look away, even though it would have made life so much easier if she could have done, and she experienced anew the sudden wild urge to throw herself at him and kiss him senseless, just to avoid hearing what he had to say. Well, not just for that reason, but it would certainly distract him. And her.

"No, I've no idea," she stalled, knowing he didn't believe her.

His blond eyebrow lifted again, impatiently, and the small gesture irked her just enough to release her from his spell. "Enlighten me," she said, letting her hand rest still in his, even though it was an effort.

Nick gave the slightest of shrugs. "Okay."

He sounded both resigned and wary. Braced, waiting for the bombshell. Just as she was. "Carlo has always wanted you and I to marry. So has Clive. They've been scheming for it to happen for years, even despite the gap in our ages." He paused, his long thumb moving delicately against the back of her hand, as if he were a trainer soothing a skittish, highly-strung animal. "So I've come here to see if we can at least *appear* to grant them their fondest wish." The thumb stilled, and so did the thick, tension-laden air in the room. Maybe even time itself had come to a halt.

"So, will you put aside our...well, shall we say our *difficulties* and become engaged to me?"

# Chapter Two

"You are joking, right?"

Panic flared in Anna's eyes for perhaps a quarter of a second, only to be extinguished almost immediately with a cool, suspicious frown. Nick hadn't expected his idea to be an easy sell, but against the odds, he'd fantasized about an immediate positive reaction.

Which obviously, he wasn't going to get. *Maledizione!* She was so poised and in control nowadays. Far more buttoned up than she once was. He wondered sourly if associating with dull, safe men had suppressed her natural wild streak as well as her sometimes fiery temper.

If so, it was high time he rescued her from that, even if only for the duration of a temporary arrangement.

"On the contrary, I'm completely serious." He allowed Anna to extricate her hand from his, half fearing that she might wipe her fingers on her fetching silky dress to wipe his touch away. She didn't, but her eyes were still wary. "I've never been more serious in my life," he added.

Those green eyes, once so hot and full of passion, narrowed. "Well, in that case, I think you're completely mad."

Feeling the stirrings of anger and frustration, Nick still had to admire her measured, even tone. Her control, and the way she skirted around derision but didn't descend to it, had a startling and very visceral effect on him. He imagined what it would be like to crack such control, in bed, and make her moan.

*Careful. Stay cool. Maintain your own control, man.*

It was hellishly difficult though, when suddenly and painfully, he wanted her more than he'd ever done before.

"Why would you say that?"

Projecting nonchalance he wasn't feeling, he lounged back against the upholstery, the thinking part of his mind trying the time-honored trick of focusing on figures, balance sheets, fiscal projections. Anything rather than fly back to that night at the Villa Rosa and the heat and scent of their coupling in his bedroom.

Which would make him hard again.

Anna laughed. Nervously? Feeling perverse, Nick hoped so.

"We've barely seen each other for four years, Nick. Isn't it going to look a bit peculiar if we're suddenly engaged?" She seemed calm, but at the same time, she was rubbing obsessively at the edge of one of her fingernails, as if intent on a flaw in her shimmering rosy nail lacquer. "Not to mention the fact we've both been seeing other people." She paused, pursed her lips for a moment. "Quite a few other people in your case." Impatiently, she abandoned the fingernail as if she'd just realized she was exhibiting a poker tell. "And as I remember the last time we were actually alone together, in what could generally be termed an intimate situation, we didn't part all that well, if you remember?"

"How could I forget?"

Base machismo surged in his gut, slipping its leash. She was fraying around the edges just a bit, he could tell, and suddenly a deep, pain-soaked part of him was glad of a reaction in her rather than the cool self-possession.

But when a veil of soft pink blush gathered across her porcelain cheekbones and developed across her throat and her cleavage, his own composure began to fracture. Her beautifully rounded breasts rose and fell beneath the thin fabric of her delicate *eau de nil* silk and lace dress, pure provocation as she clearly fought for equilibrium.

On his feet without conscious thought, he resumed his pacing. He didn't want her to look at him too closely and see his erection. It was much easier for women, if they were aroused it wasn't as obvious, and that gave them an advantage. How could he work through the justification of his plan, especially when it was so vaguely thought out in his own mind, if he was sporting a raging hard-on and she was looking at it?

*I should have known this would happen. I got stiff looking at her picture, how in God's name could I avoid it seeing her for real, touching her skin, smelling her scent?*

At the window, Nick stared out into the damp garden and composed himself. They'd have to get past that night at villa. Their elephant in the room. It was no good thinking they could go on ignoring what had happened. Perhaps they'd been fools to blank it from their lives for so long?

Especially as it was the most defining event of his life.

Could that be true? No, it couldn't. It mustn't.

The illumination, sudden and sharp, swept through him, bringing confusion in its wake that was so unlike his usual hard-focused clarity. Aware she might think he was crazy, he shook his head to clear it, but couldn't do away with the sense of sand shifting beneath his feet.

*Concentrate. Stay on message. Remember the plan. Remember the way you conduct your life.*

Whirling around, marshalling the steel and purpose that usually served him so well in business, he said, "We have to

33

talk about that night, Anna. We've danced around it since it happened and it'll only fester if we leave it any longer."

"What's to discuss?" Anna held his gaze, and the lack of fear in her eyes was awesome, almost warrior. He wasn't the only one who'd pulled himself together. "I made a mistake...and you informed me of it in no uncertain terms. There's nothing more to be said." Her voice was steady, but huskier than before. And the blush in her cheeks was pinker, hotter.

Oh hell, he wanted her more than ever.

"It was a lot more than that. And we need to talk about it." He moved to push his hands in his pockets, then thought better of it and crossed his arms in front of him.

Suddenly, Anna was on her feet, fists clenched at her sides. "Yes, there was a bit in the middle that you seemed to enjoy— quite a lot as I recall! But after that, all I remember is you suddenly turning into the Reverend Father of Good Sense and Moral Rectitude and preaching me a sermon along the lines of 'You young idiot!' and 'How could you be so stupid?' and *'Per Dio*, what on earth were you thinking?'"

*Per Dio* indeed! That night he'd lost his cool completely, just as he was in serious danger of losing it now.

There had been a delicious, drowsy awakening, then shocked realization, then an almost fatalistic slide into the most soul-drenching pleasure. And afterwards, another rollercoaster plunge, but this time into another realization. The fact that he'd just had sex with exactly the type of woman, exactly *the* woman whom he shouldn't have allowed himself anywhere near.

Remorse had shocked him in its agonizing intensity. Anna hadn't been one of his no-strings sophisticates who knew the score. Not then, and maybe not now. His plan was stupid...stupid, but he couldn't forget the way his father's weary eyes burned with hope at the mention of her name.

And yet, there was the other thing too. The need to get past that night, exorcise their demons and move on properly. Surely she wanted the same? Or was he just fooling himself so he had an excuse to bed her again? His thoughts whirled, round and round, and his temples ached from the urge to shake his head again.

"I was harsh. I shouldn't have been. I admit that." It seemed a hollow concession at best, and he hated the memory of her lovely face crumpling in distress.

"And presumptuous," she flung back at him, "and arrogant."

"Okay, yes, it was arrogant of me to presume that because you wanted to fuck me you'd expect me to get into a serious relationship with you afterwards." Odd voices, yearnings, muttered in his head. "And it was a shock realizing you were a virgin...it was...was a responsibility."

"Which you don't like. I know that. I only wanted to get rid of my virginity with a man I knew was likely to be pretty damn good in bed." Anna's delicate chin came up as she spoke. Her expression was determined and brittle and he didn't like it at all. "I picked you because I knew you were a player and you could get the job done."

Sudden outrage barreled through him, but at her or himself, he wasn't quite sure. Nevertheless it swept aside all better judgment and pragmatism. It was one thing to have a reputation as a seasoned stud—deserved, admittedly—but to be told he'd been chosen purely as a stallion hurt like a punch in the gut. Especially as he still wasn't sure she was telling the truth.

He wanted a drink. He wanted to clear his head, which was suddenly aching. He wanted release, and whether it was emotional or just pure sex, he didn't care.

"Well, in view of the fact that I never asked you for specifics at the time...was I satisfactory?" he demanded, "Did I 'get the job done', as you so delicately put it?"

To his surprise, Anna laughed. A light, sexy laugh that should have broken the tension, but didn't. "Nick! You are kidding, aren't you? If you couldn't tell from all the—" her eyes skittered away just a second, and she swallowed furiously, "—all the fuss I made, then you obviously aren't the all-conquering sexual love-rat everyone believes you to be."

"Reports of my sexual prowess have been greatly exaggerated," he murmured dryly, but inside he found a smile, stupidly pleased at the idea of "getting the job done" and well.

Because she'd pleased him. *Per Dio*, how she'd pleased him. He'd never had quite the same sublime experience since, and he'd had lovers who were world-class beauties, sexually voracious and practiced seductresses to boot.

Looking down at Anna's face, he saw courage and fire in every perfect contour. Her mouth was luscious yet determined and her eyes held his, not quailing, not hiding anything.

She *did* want him, but she was wary. Her slender body had an almost feline quality of readiness, as if she were gathering herself to dart away from him if he made the slightest wrong move. Either that or she was poised to attack him. Even ravish him.

But everything about her made him want to launch his own counterattack. To haul her against him and kiss her until the last sub-atomic particle of hostility in her had melted and she was eager and aroused in his arms. As eager and aroused as he was.

Instead, he dropped onto the sofa again, taking care to observe her personal space while every fiber of his being howled at him to invade it. "Is that what you think of me? That I'm a love-rat?" He patted the seat beside him, and felt a ridiculous, almost boyish happiness when she sat too.

He recognized his peril when close proximity surrounded him with the delicate drift of her perfume. It was very light, yet as rich as a basket of summer flowers, and it was exactly the same fragrance she'd worn in bed at Villa Rosa. It had been the only thing she'd been wearing that night and it had filled his head with madness.

As it did now.

"It's a pretty crude way of putting it, but essentially...yes." She glanced down at his thigh, and hers, almost touching, and he could tell she wanted to move, but he wasn't quite sure whether away or closer. "According to those—" she nodded to a pile of shiny magazines lying on the nearby coffee table, "—and what everybody says, you do seem to work your way through a lot of women."

"So you believe the made-up tales of trashy magazines and evil-minded gossips?" he murmured, irrationally wounded, but knowing he shouldn't blame her. He as good as promoted that image of himself, so his lovers wouldn't be cruelly disappointed when forever wasn't on offer. "I've always credited you with more intelligence than that, Anna."

Nick felt an intense desire to defend himself. Take her by the shoulders, look deep into her intelligent green eyes and convince her by sheer force of personality that he wasn't the unprincipled womanizer the sensationalist press and his self-created persona portrayed him to be. But what would be the point of that? She was safer thinking he *was* a womanizer. At least that way she knew where she stood.

"I enjoy women," he conceded, "And I enjoy variety. But I don't set out to misrepresent myself. Every woman I sleep with knows the score. No strings. No commitment. No wedding bells.

Long-term relationships and me aren't a viable mixture, Anna. Haven't I always told you that?"

Anna's eyes narrowed again, and her brow pleated beneath her feathery blonde fringe. "And yet you're asking me to marry you."

He'd almost forgotten what he was here for. Her intimate proximity, her scent, the reality of her unique beauty... It was difficult to stay on message this close to her.

"No." Starkly, he dragged himself back to his purpose. "What I'm asking you is that you become *engaged* to me. Just that, and for a strictly limited period. If Carlo thinks he's got his wish, it will give him just the boost he needs to start fighting back to health."

Momentarily, he saw the dull exhaustion in his father's eyes. And then, the older man's entire face aglow on hearing that all his hints and urgings with respect to the girl he most wanted as a daughter-in-law were finally set to be fulfilled. For the first time in days, there'd been real strength and vigor when Carlo had embraced him.

"So it'd all be an empty façade?"

She was frowning again. Always frowning. He wanted to kiss the porcelain-pale skin of her forehead and smooth away her suspicion.

"A fiction. For a good cause."

There was a long silence. The scheme had made perfect sense when he'd formulated it in a flash of inspiration at his father's bedside. But confronted with Anna, on whom it all hinged, it sounded as if he'd lost his mind, not to mention all sense of the judgment and savvy he prided himself on.

The moments stretched on, and finally, Nick lost patience, with himself as much as with Anna.

"Well? Will you do it?" he demanded, "Aren't you going to answer?"

What could she answer? The whirl of a million conflicting feelings contrasted starkly with the slow, steady tick of the antique grandfather clock in the corner of the room.

*Focus, woman! Think. Breathe. Don't let him see that you're in a flat spin and don't know what to think or do.*

But it was a tough task, especially with Nick so close and looking and smelling and sounding so good. He'd always been as handsome as a fallen angel and he just seemed to get more attractive and sexually irresistible with every year that passed. She should have distance and self-control and a resistance to him after all this time, but it just seemed more impossible than ever. Especially as she sensed there was even more to his preposterous suggestion than the dramatic performance of the fake engagement.

"You don't expect me to answer right now, do you?" She met those blue, blue eyes as coolly as she could. "It needs at least a bit of mulling over. You must at least allow me that."

"Carlo isn't getting any better, Anna."

Oh, so cold all of a sudden. It was like a rabbit punch, but he was right, of course. She saw Carlo's craggy face for a moment—always smiling, always kind and always generous. She'd been planning to fly to Italy as soon as he came off the critical list and could see visitors.

"Yes, I know that. Do you think I don't care?" she flung out, "I'm certainly a lot more concerned about his welfare than I am about yours."

*Idiot. Don't antagonize him. Things are sticky enough already.*

"Then say yes for him, not me." There was no getting around him. He was determined. And when Nick set his mind on something he'd always got his way. His will was as steely and unyielding as his superbly muscled body.

*No, don't think about his body!*

"I need a little time, Nick. I won't be coerced." In an attempt to distract him, she shot to her feet again. "But I won't keep you waiting long." She fixed her eyes on the door and her path of escape, back to the party.

In what seemed only the blink of an eye, he was on his feet too, blocking that path.

"Very well, Anna," he murmured. He was average tall, but not massive, and yet he seemed to loom over her in a way that was completely and unequivocally male. "But not too long, eh?" He tilted his head, and the light from the chandelier above seemed to turn his blond hair to some fabulous mystical metal. One long-fingered hand reached out and touched her cheek, and it felt like a brand. His mark. On her.

"Thank you, *cara mia.*" His voice was soft, almost sweet, but the addition of the Italian endearment was a subtle taunt. "But there's one little complication you need to attend to, I think."

"What's that?" She watched his mouth, and the insolent curve of his full lower lip, as she waited for enlightenment. Or something.

"Don't you have a boyfriend, Anna?"

*Oh hell, Martin.*

Nick's smile broadened. He was hugely amused by the fact she obviously hadn't given Martin a single thought since she'd opened the door. Admittedly, she and Martin were only casual, and she'd decided not to keep stringing him along because it wasn't fair to him...but still. How could she forget him completely? That was awful.

"My real relationships are no business whatsoever of yours, Nick." She looked at him boldly, chin up. It would have been easier if he wasn't still touching her, but she couldn't seem to move her head and shake him off. "You'd better concern yourself only with this false one. *If* I decide to go through with it."

Irked by his grin, she held his gaze and was rewarded by a faint flash of irritation in Nick's eyes. "And anyway, how do you know whether I'm seeing anyone or not? Have you been spying on me?"

Nick's fingers were like five burning points against the skin of her cheek, and they curved slightly as if coaxing her closer. "I have my sources." His voice was a low, thrilling whisper, and his eyes were fixed on her mouth. To her consternation, Anna imagined she could actually feel the scrutiny, a tingling sensation that made her lips more sensitive, redder and more enticing.

*Don't be mental. You're imagining things. Just back away and make a dignified break for the party. Do it now!*

But it was as if she was trapped in some kind of warm, delicious and infinitely pleasant-feeling glue. Her body was immobilized, her senses intoxicated. Nick's own mouth tempted her like chocolate or some luscious tropical fruit, primal and sinful.

"Is that how thrilling he is?" Nick breathed, "Five minutes with me and you completely forget he exists?"

"No! That's not true."

The words were hollow and she hardly had the strength to get them out. Nick was so close they were sharing the same oxygen, and his spicy cologne invaded her mind like dark alchemy.

"Oh, it is, *tesoro mio*, it surely is." His words faded to a sultry murmur as he angled his gilded head and brought his lips down slowly and with complete confidence on hers.

The pressure was so gentle, like velvet gliding over her lips. His taste was so sweet—as mind-altering as the smell of him—and it compelled her to succumb. In one last defensive gesture, she put up a hand, fingers spread against his chest with the intention of pushing him away. But a moment later both her hands were sliding around his back of their own volition to hold on tightly to him as if her very life depended on it.

And all the time his eyes were open, intent on hers, darkened to the intense midnight hue of a moonless night. Stunned by their power, Anna let her own lids flutter closed.

And when his mobile, questing tongue sought entrance into her mouth, it was as if all the interminable years apart had disappeared, counting for nothing. She was back with him in his bed, naked and free, their bodies pressed together inch for inch. In a weird confluence of past and present, she seemed to feel every contour of his musculature, the very heat of his satin skin, the fierce insistence of his erection against her belly.

Which was no fantasy.

Anna's eyes flew open and she jerked, but Nick slid his arms around her and held her closer than ever. Bizarrely, the firm hold soothed her sudden panic and it was easy, oh so easy to succumb to him.

Their tongues darted against each other, playing and challenging, Anna giving back now as good as she got, reveling in the thrills. She heard—and felt—Nick laugh deep in his throat, but the kisses were so delicious that she couldn't be bothered to get angry with him. Couldn't be bothered to do anything other than what came perfectly naturally, which was to circle her belly against his loins, hungry and wanton.

"Anna," he groaned, wrenching his lips from hers and burying them in her hair, "I've spent four whole years wondering if you'd still feel like this." His fingers massaged her spine, then slid lower, compelling her sex closer to his.

Anna's eyes prickled. Her name sounded so different on his lips when he was aroused. The way he spoke normally was almost completely accentless and English, but when he muttered, "Anna" again, it sounded as Latin and romantic as high opera, and at the same time, tender and intimate.

Her softly breathed name had been on his lips as he'd entered her body. She remembered the fleeting jolt of pain, his moment of hesitation, and then the awesome sensation of being filled and possessed by him, at last. Reaching up to touch his face, she urged his mouth back down on hers, then wound her fingers into his thick, damp hair, relishing its silkiness and the wild way it curled.

Holding him, savoring the taste of his mouth and the feel of his lean, potent body against her, Anna wanted the kiss to go on forever. Like this, there were no issues between them, no problems, no history. They were just male and female, meant for each other, perfectly matched.

Then the creak of the library door and an exaggerated stage cough snapped the spell, and everything was pretty much wrong again. Anna shot away from Nick and whirled around to see her father standing in the doorway, his jolly, jowly face pink above his bow tie and dress shirt and a pleased-as-punch grin plastered across it.

"Nick! How good to see you, my boy," Clive Felgate exclaimed, striding forward. "I'm so glad you could make it." He grabbed Nick's hand and pumped it for dear life, slapping the younger man on the arm as if he'd just scored a winning goal or come first in a marathon. "I hope this means that Carlo is doing much better?"

Still reeling from the kiss, Anna hung away from the two of them, relieved to be ignored for a second or two. She needed breathing space to compose herself. Nick, she noted, didn't appear to need time out. He'd segued instantly into comfortable bonhomie with her father, as easily if Clive had found them discussing the weather. Smiling and relaxed, he chatted easily about Carlo and congratulated Clive on his birthday.

"I have a gift from Carlo and myself, but it's slightly too large to have brought it along tonight." Despite the fact that Nick infuriated her, Anna had to admit to a genuine gratitude as he told her father about the gift, a watercolor by one of his favorite artists. The way Clive's face lit up was enough for her to cut Nick a fair bit of slack. Her father's recent money problems, which he'd refused to discuss with her, had suppressed his naturally cheerful nature, so it warmed her heart to see him smiling and excited like this. Nick's gift—both extravagant and thoughtfully chosen—had lifted his spirits no end.

But was it just the watercolor? She suspected not, shuddering at implications that alarmed her. Clive had been grinning like a loon already when he'd happened upon them. The wink and the encouraging look her father flashed her over Nick's shoulder only confirmed her worst fears.

*Oh no! You haven't said anything to my dad already, have you, Nick Lisitano? Please don't tell me you've told him you're proposing...*

To Clive it didn't matter she'd been seeing Martin. Her father adored Nick, and always had done, and without being overtly hostile, he'd made it plain he wasn't impressed with Martin and thought him dull.

"Thank you, my boy. You're far too generous," Clive went on, shaking Nick's hand anew, then suddenly laughing and shrugging and giving him the sort of bear hug he'd definitely give a prospective son-in-law. Nick was the son Clive had never had, and, even though Anna knew he loved her unstintingly, had always wanted. It warmed her heart to see the fondness between the two men, but at the same time, she felt doubly angry with Nick for raising her dad's hopes with his blatantly false charade.

*Oh, this is such a mess. It'll end in tears.* She manufactured a smile as Clive gestured for her to join them. *And maybe not just mine, by the look of it.*

If a party could be judged to be both roaring success and an unmitigated disaster, this was it, Anna decided a while later as she circulated, clutching an untouched glass of champagne in her hand like a fragile lifebelt.

The volume of conversation and civilized laughter was bouncing cheerfully off the walls and the supplies of hors d'ouvres, champagne and cocktails were holding up well despite the arrival of several more guests than had been expected for the sit-down dinner to follow.

With a fake grin, Anna stared across the room, where the one guest she still wished hadn't arrived was holding forth to a couple of adoring, simpering older women. Nick looked like a renaissance prince with his own personal court of cooing matrons, she observed grimly. He was just shameless. He clearly couldn't resist turning the charm on full beam.

*You really think you're God's gift to womanhood, don't you?*

Hurling a quiver of silent daggers at him, she flushed pink when he glanced back at her, his knowing smirk suggesting he might have heard her thoughts.

*You arrogant monster!* She only just stopped herself

mouthing the words when he flashed her a hint of a wink.

"They don't call him The Golden Italian for nothing, do they?" said a voice in her ear, and she turned to find Lydia, her aunt, also studying the sight of Nick and his impromptu mini-harem. "Lord, if I were twenty years younger I'd take a crack at him myself," Lydia sighed, quaffing quickly from her glass of champagne. "Not that he'd even look at me... He has other interests," she intoned, tapping the side of her nose.

"What, you mean shagging half the actresses and most of the supermodels in Europe?" snipped Anna, turning her back on the source of her ire to give Lydia her full attention. "Hey, I've got a bone to pick with you. Himself over there seems to know all about me and Martin and he says he's got 'sources'. What have you been telling him? How come he's so *au fait* with my love life all of a sudden?"

"What love life?" said Lydia dismissively. "You don't count that uptight little mummy's boy Martin as a love life, do you? Because if you do, you should seriously rethink your idea of what constitutes a lover, my sweet."

Lydia paused to wave to Nick across the room, champagne sloshing dangerously as she did. "*That's* what a lover should look like, pet. And the sooner you realize that the better."

"Martin is very—" a suitable adjective eluded her, "—very nice." How half-hearted did that sound? "And of course Nick looks like a lover. He's a serial womanizer with all the moral fiber of a wild boar in rut. What else would he look like?" She leant forward, trying to get Lydia back on track. "And that still doesn't answer my question. What have you been telling Nick about me?"

"You mean what has he been asking?" Lydia grew more serious. "I've no idea what happened between the two of you four years ago, but I know something did...and ever since then, he's been coming to me regularly to find out what's going on with you. I told him not to be an idiot and to ask you himself, but it seems where you and he are concerned, he's just as ridiculous as you are."

The room was warm, but still Anna shivered. What was the hell was Nick up to monitoring her like that? He'd made it known in the plainest of terms that night at Villa Rosa he wasn't interested in her romantically, so why continue to check up on her?

"Nothing happened between us," she said, tamping down her irritation with Lydia. Her aunt was the most well-meaning person on the face of the earth, and clearly thought she'd been acting in the best of interests. "I think Nick and I have just sort of outgrown each other over the years. I did have a crush on him at one time, but we've both found new friends, new interests."

Was he still watching her? Her body seemed to think so. She had visible goose bumps on her arms, and unless it was due to some unexpected adulterant in the champagne that was affecting them, her lips were still tingling from that kiss.

Lydia snorted and said a rude word. There was no fooling her, even when Anna realized she'd sort of managed to fool herself. Almost... "If he's outgrown you, why on earth did he—" She stopped short, then bit her lip as Anna focused on her. "Look forget it. Let's enjoy the party."

"Why on earth did he what?" Anna demanded. What had Nick done? What on earth had he done?

"Nothing," persisted Lydia.

"Tell me, Lyd! If it's to do with me, I've a right to know."

Her aunt had the decency to look shamefaced, but she stopped prevaricating. "Well, he offered to invest in Traditional Temps, that's what. He knew how important the business is to you, and he wanted to ensure we got off to a good start."

"Oh, please don't tell me you accepted and pretended that it was your own money." Agitation swirled in Anna's throat. The idea of Nick exerting control over the only thing she considered to be truly hers—the business she and Lydia had started together—was deeply unnerving, almost horrifying. His Machiavellian schemes were extending into all corners of her life, it seemed.

"No, of course not," said Lydia, shaking her head. "For one thing I wouldn't be able to fake the sort of funds Nick was offering. And two, I knew you wouldn't accept it—for some reason best known to yourself—so I declined." Her eyes brightened. "But he did say the offer would always be on the table if we changed our minds."

Anna sighed. "I'll take that under advisement," she said dryly, then turned around, only to find, of course, that Nick was still watching her closely. His slight, insolent smile only increased her disquiet and made her even more convinced that he'd acquired demonic powers somewhere along the line and could read her mind.

If only she could charge across and have the whole business out with him, here and now. But it was her dad's party, and the last thing she wanted was a scene. But as dinner was announced, the temptation to confront Nick still simmered in her gut.

*Oh, why does this not surprise me?*

Lydia had clearly rigged the place settings too. There was no other logical explanation for finding herself sitting next to Nick. Summoning a fair attempt at a carefree, convivial, dinner-party smile, she allowed him to draw out her seat for her, then tuck it neatly behind her knees when she sat. Anticipating a frontal conversation attack, she braced herself, but was saved his individual attention by the guest on his other side. A large, over-dressed, over-made-up, over-perfumed woman, the wife of one of her father's many friends, engaged Nick in animated conversation and a display of her ample cleavage.

*Enjoy!* thought Anna savagely, knowing it was only a matter of time before her turn came.

"So, Anna, is Traditional Temps thriving?"

Nick's voice was casual, social and warm, but beneath the surface it was loaded and provocative. Ding dong went the warning bell in Anna's brain.

She turned to look at him and found his beautiful eyes scoping her out, assessing, monitoring. It was blatantly obvious he knew that she knew.

Anna kept her voice even and low, grappling not to reveal any hint of antagonism. "You tell me, Nick," she observed, "It seems you know more about my life these days than I do. Both business and personal."

He had the grace to look perplexed for a microsecond, but when he answered, his tone was as unabashed, unrepentant.

"Busted." He put up his hands in a quick, graceful gesture of surrender.

"Why, Nick? Why spy on me?" she murmured, leaning back to let one of the hired waitresses take her barely touched plate.

"What you so dramatically call spying is merely concerned interest, Anna. Don't you follow the course of my life too? You admitted yourself that you're an avid reader of magazine articles."

Heat blossomed in Anna's face. If Lydia had revealed to him the extent of her obsession with the celebrity press, and the way it so often featured him, there was little point in denying it.

"I never said 'avid', and I only read those things because the mind boggles, wondering whatever you're going to get up to next. Or who you're going to get up to it with. There doesn't seem to be a single high-profile woman on two continents that you haven't been linked with."

"Oh, that again." He gave a cool little shake of his shining head. "It seems to me that you're far more interested in my love life than I am myself."

By rights, it should have been Anna's turn to say busted and backtrack gracefully, but she couldn't.

"The whole world can't help but follow your love life, Nick. Those pictures at the Cannes Film Festival with Maria Rossi all over you like a rash...well, they were borderline pornographic."

And those photos had hurt. Seeing Nick with Italy's hottest and most beautiful young actress entwined around him had been a shock, inducing a reaction that Anna didn't want to think about.

Nick remained unfazed.

"You're exaggerating, Anna. And anyway, Maria is Italian, and we Italians tend towards the demonstrative. Don't you and your *adorato* Johnson ever show affection to each other in public?"

Red mist floated in front of Anna's eyes, and she wanted to say a very bad word and tell him it was none of his business. He'd hit a particular nerve with stinging accuracy. Martin was reserved and a little old-fashioned, and not prone to demonstrating his feelings. It was one of the main reasons she'd come to the conclusion they were completely unsuited, should go their separate ways and both be happier and better off. She longed for a touch, a possessive kiss that others might see, and unfortunately, much as she tried to deny it, her heart knew from whom she wanted those touches and kisses. Worse, she knew that if Martin had been anything like Nick, nothing on earth could have stopped him from publicly proclaiming she was his, almost caveman style.

*Don't go there!*

Drawing in a deep, invisible breath, she searched for a calm centre. The only thing for it was a radical change of tack.

"Why did you offer to invest in my business, Nick?" she questioned in an undertone, "Looking for a way to get control over me or something?"

"God, you're a cantankerous woman, Anna." There was a silvery edge of exasperation in his voice that made Anna feel aggressive and guilty, yet at the same time a tiny bit pleased with herself. So, the mighty Niccolo Lisitano wasn't completely unflappable after all. "Can't you just believe that I wanted to help you? Without strings?"

"No. I can't."

Doggedly, she glanced around to make sure that curious ears were not tuned their way, "You're devious, Nick, and you're a power-tripper. And I know you're not averse to underhanded tactics if they'll get you what you want."

Nick took a sip from his water glass before he replied. "And I'm not the only one," he said, soft and low and sexy, his eyes darker now, full of sensuality and thrilling masculine threat.

Anna's silver fork clattered onto her plate and everybody did look their way.

Was he never, ever going to let her forget that night? Was she going to have to suffer to the end of her days for once being young and foolhardy and head over heels in puppy lust with him?

It seemed that way.

"I'm sorry, *cara*, but you asked for it."

Dripping with double meaning, his silky tone seemed to vibrate through Anna's nerves as he reached for her hand and held it. The contact was feather-light, but infinitely unsettling.

"When I offered to invest it was a genuine offer of help. There was no agenda." His fingertips moved, ever so slightly, and Anna felt butterflies the size of golden eagles cavorting around in her chest. "What kind of a man do you think I am that I would try to leverage you that way?"

The butterflies, and her heart, bashed wildly against her breastbone. Maybe she had misjudged him? Maybe she was overreacting? Summoning her courage, she met his gaze boldly, searching for clues.

The moment of dark, sexual threat seemed to be gone. His smile was open, guileless, almost gentle.

And yet...and yet... Surely he knew what effect the touch of his hand was having on her? All the time he was playing his Mr. Sincerity act, he was employing the dirtiest of lowdown tactics to confuse her and slyly impose his will on her.

"I don't know what kind of a man you are, Nick."

Her response was slow, and she was worried that the faint, almost reedy note in her voice gave her away. She had to pull herself together and not let him get to her. "In fact, I'm not sure I've ever known. I thought I did once, but then you confounded me. I...I..." She turned away, longing to snatch back her hand, but unable to.

*Back to that night again,* she thought in despair. Would its thousand-mile shadow ever lift from her life and let her forget?

"I was wrong. I admit that," Nick said quietly, "Can't you forgive me? Let it rest? So we can start again now and do something worthwhile?"

His voice was so beguiling that Anna felt her defenses disintegrating. Then a second later, there was the purest shock

52

as he spoke again, his voice crisp and decisive. "Let's talk later. This is Clive's party. It's neither the place nor time to debate the past...or the future."

Anna's head shot up and she snatched a glance at him. And saw him looking not at her, but at the table beyond. One or two of the other guests were still observing them, clearly straining their ears to the limit to follow their exchange. Even though she and Nick had kept their voices low, their body language must have been semaphoring the conflict between them.

"Of course."

Reacquiring her bright smile and nodding to one or two people before returning her attention towards Nick, she continued quietly, "You're right. This isn't the place."

With a quick squeeze, Nick released her hand, and against everything that was good sense, Anna felt instantly bereft.

"But we will talk." His tone was hushed, but he was making a statement of intent, not asking a question.

*Oh yes we will, unfortunately,* thought Anna as she nodded, not relishing the prospect of stirring things better left unstirred.

# Chapter Three

At last the party was over and Anna tried to relax and reflect on the general success of the evening, but Nick's words "we will talk" tolled in her head like a Gothic church bell in an old black and white horror movie.

At least he was back at the Savoy now, and the talk would be postponed for a few hours. Grateful for time to regroup, Anna found herself physically gasping with relief, and then told herself not to be such a ridiculous drama queen. For Carlo's sake, she had no option but to give Nick a quick answer, but at least she had a few hours tonight to gather her wits.

The raft of post-party chores proved distracting and Anna bade farewell to the catering staff, tipping them lavishly for a job well done. She also insisted, despite strong protest, that their housekeeper, Mrs. Brewster take a paid day or two off to compensate her for her Herculean efforts during the run up to the party.

Less easy to deal with was Anna's promise to give Lydia a full and frank report on "the Nick situation".

Luckily, her aunt's partiality for champagne had got the better of her, and the way Lydia shambled uncertainly into a taxi, with a vague and giggly good night, gave Anna just the respite she needed on that score too. Grinning wryly, she had a distinct feeling that Lydia would be a no show at Traditional

Temps in the morning.

Finally, with the house empty, Anna returned to the front hall, planning to pop in on her father while he took his customary nightcap in the library.

But the hall yielded a shock.

*Oh, for heaven's sake, no!*

Still hanging on the coat rack was a rather beautiful and unmistakable black cashmere overcoat, and on the floor beside it, a discreetly expensive overnight case had materialized from somewhere.

*Why are you still here?*

As if in answer, the sound of convivial male conversation drifted from the library. One voice was Nick's, deep, assured, ever-confident—the other was her father's, sounding almost boyish with happiness and excitement.

*Uh oh, why so chipper, Dad?*

A sneaking sense of dread clutched at Anna's heart, making her feel disorientated.

No! He couldn't have! Not without "the talk". Not without consulting her first.

For a moment, genuine faintness gripped Anna's entire body, but then she squashed it down ruthlessly, gritting her teeth and clenching her fists. Righteous anger boiled away the final fragments.

*You always get what you want, don't you, Nick?*

Tamping down her inner comparisons of the various methods of murder and dismemberment, she strode towards the doorway. *Once you only wanted to get rid of me, and you did it without turning even one hair on your shining, arrogant head. Now, you expect me to fall in with your schemes without a single proviso of my own. And you've launched a pre-emptive strike so I don't have choice in the matter!*

It was no comfort at all that she'd already resolved to go through with the charade for the sake of Carlo. Nick's high-handed action had removed her last opportunity to lay down her own ground rules first.

*Game on, you sneaky arrogant swine!* Lifting her chin, she entered the library and the atmosphere of warm, male companionship and mutual backslapping.

Her father was happily installed in his favorite wing chair, and Nick was lounging on the chesterfield, his suit jacket flung across the back of it and his dark collar and tie casually loosened. Each man had a snifter of brandy to hand on a side table.

"My darling, why didn't you tell me?" Clive sprang out of his chair with more speed and vigor than she'd seen in him in a long time, and almost threw himself across the room to embrace her. His crushing hug left her in no doubt that her worst fears had been realized.

"You're such a sly boots, love," he remonstrated, freeing her, his face ruddy with unadulterated joy. "I didn't even realize that you and Nick had been seeing each other, and here he is, doing the old-fashioned thing and asking for your hand in marriage." Clive reached for the said hand and squeezed it passionately, "I've said yes, of course, love, so no worries on that score."

*He's never looked this happy before in his life,* Anna thought, desperately manufacturing a smile commensurate with a joyous engagement. It would be cruel to spoil her dad's elation with a lack of enthusiasm.

Yet all the time, her attention gravitated like a magnet towards the tall figure of Nick, who'd unwound himself gracefully from the sofa and was walking towards her.

Swimming panic lurched around in her midsection, but with a supreme effort, she forced her frozen grin into a facsimile of a loving fiancée's greeting.

"Oh, you know me, Dad." It was a battle royal, but she got the words out in a convincing, cheerful fashion. Even though every nerve-end was pinging now that Nick's left arm had slid possessively around her waist. "I like to keep things quiet until I know for sure."

The light but insistent pressure of strong male fingertips against her rib cage seemed to impress upon her the need to stay firmly on message.

"But has there ever been any doubt, *cara mia?*" he murmured in her ear, dusting a brief kiss into her hair.

*Well, I've got mountains of it! Oceans of it!*

Anna felt as if she were being crushed by a velvet vise, slowly and inexorably. Clive was clearly ecstatic over the prospect of his new son-in-law. How were they ever going to get out of this one without eventually disappointing him? And Carlo, for that matter? This might be a long, long haul if Nick's father took time to fully recover.

"Well, it's a relief to know that it isn't Martin Johnson!" pronounced her father roundly, retrieving his brandy for a celebratory swig. "Can't see what you ever saw in him." He winked. "But that's just you being a crafty little monkey, I guess. Martin Johnson was just a smokescreen so you could surprise your old dad with the real news." He beamed so widely that Anna feared his face might split.

"Er...something like that."

Nick's *fait accompli* was going to make it even more awkward to effect an amiable break-up with Martin. Guilt engulfed her. For all his faults, Martin was a decent sort of guy and didn't deserve this pantomime dropped on him like an anvil. At best, he'd think she'd gone off her head.

"But Martin's really a very nice man," she continued, her mind whirling as the fingertip pressure on her waist suddenly increased. Five points of fire were burning into her skin through the silk of her dress. A fire that expunged all thoughts of Martin and replaced them with the incandescent image of the beautiful, confident man at her side. "And he's a good friend," she added defiantly, trying to edge sideways without her father noticing.

"That's as maybe." Clive dismissed Martin with a last sip of his brandy before setting the glass aside, "But the important news is you and Nick, my dear." He strode forward again, grasped Nick's free right hand and shook it enthusiastically, then stretched his arms round the both of them and hugged them, "I couldn't be happier. Really," he finished gruffly, his eyes suspiciously bright.

*Oh hell!*

Anna felt teary herself at the thought of Clive's reaction to the eventual conclusion of this charade. Martin wasn't the only one in line for an anvil. The iniquity of Nick imposing this insane scheme on them made her want to stomp down hard on his foot and demand to know whether he'd considered *all* its possible repercussions.

Granted, fathers both English and Italian were going to be over the moon in the short term…but in the longer term? Well, she didn't like to think about it.

But Nick's pointed smile told her she'd be wise to play along.

*4.20 a.m.*

Anna glared at her bedside clock's illuminated display with gritty eyes that felt as if they hadn't closed once since she'd finally escaped to her room.

Dealing with her dad's unabashed delight and Nick's steady, watchful triumph whilst striving to project a blissful fiancée image had been exhausting. But now she was in bed sleep comprehensively eluded her.

"Oh for crying out loud!"

Sitting up, she sighed and rubbed her eyes with the heels of her hands. What a mess. If only she could turn back time and run the evening in an entirely different way.

Just a few hours ago, she'd been happily in control of her life, running a successful, satisfying business. Okay, she'd been slightly worried about breaking up with a man who was nice and companionable, but not very exciting. But when they were amicably parted, her future had looked pretty tranquil and mapped out.

Now everything was part of a roiling emotional weather system with Niccolo Lisitano slap-bang in the centre of its still, deceptive eye. Where he seemed to be perfectly happy, even if everyone around him was in turmoil.

Rising, Anna reached for her dressing gown, but paused as she caught a glimpse of herself in her pier glass. Something like a cross between a raving red-eyed freak and a repressed maiden aunt stared back at her. She pulled a face at the oversized, rather utilitarian nightshirt she'd chosen.

Even though there was still a chill in the spring night air, conditions weren't all that Arctic. There was only one reason she'd bundled herself up from throat to ankle like this. It was psychological armor.

*And guess who I'm protecting myself from?*

She glowered at the wall, beyond which, a couple of doors

down the hall her nemesis was no doubt sleeping the sleep of the totally untroubled. He'd had his overnight bag sent round from the Savoy at the behest of her father, and she didn't like to think about what Clive was probably subconsciously hoping would happen.

The main sleep-dispelling problem was that knowing Nick was just down the hall was playing havoc with her imagination.

To her eternal cost, she knew that he always slept naked, and images of his gleaming muscular limbs, his powerful torso—and more—flooded into her mind and unleashed a riptide of alarming sensations. Gritting her teeth, she cinched the belt of her velour robe so tightly it almost choked her breathing, then with a sigh, she loosened it again.

A cup of tea. That's what she needed. The perennial English answer to stress and trauma, both of which she'd been experiencing more or less continuously since she'd first opened the front door and set eyes on Nick.

And doors, that was another thing.

Frowning, she turned the key in the lock of her bedroom door as quietly as she could. Since when had she ever locked herself in her room at night? Not once, even when she'd been going through a brief adolescent rebellion phase. Yet tonight the need for security had been instinctive, even if unnecessary. For all his wild reputation as a player, Nick also adhered to a strict Italian code of chivalry towards the female sex. He'd certainly never come to a woman's bedroom uninvited.

Which was more than she could say when the boot was on the other foot.

The familiar mix of embarrassment and anguish washed through her, the cocktail she'd lived with for four years. Surprise midnight visits were *her* prerogative.

"Never again," she muttered, unlocking the door, but

wishing she could lock up the past, and its resonances, and start afresh.

For about the hundredth time since Nick's re-entry into her life had stunned her, she commanded herself to get a grip, then padded out onto the landing, her slipper-clad feet silent on the carpet. Going downstairs to the kitchen was questionable logic, to say the least, but if she lay brooding and tossing in the darkness much longer she'd probably go completely and utterly barking mad.

In the basement passage leading to Mrs. Brewster's cozy kitchen domain, Anna came to a silent, breathless halt.

Faint sounds came from beyond the door.

The same sense of ominous pre-knowledge gripped her that she'd experienced earlier at the party. Cheerfully dismissive of energy bills and global warming, Mrs. B always left a light burning in the kitchen when she left, in case either Anna or her father wanted a hot drink in the night. Now it sounded as if somebody was in there, for just that purpose.

*It's Dad,* Anna instructed herself firmly, dismissing the idea of a burglar or other intruder because of their efficient security system.

Her gut, however, had other ideas. It, and her heart and her nerves and every molecule in her body, all knew exactly who was in the kitchen. And the urge to turn around and flee to her bedroom sent urgent messages to her feet.

Yet, irrationally, a more powerful force drove her onwards.

Fate? Curiosity? Rabid, destructive emotional death-wish? Whatever it was, Anna hovered just outside the partially open door, peering in from the cover of the shadows.

Nick had a cupboard door ajar, and with a frown on his face, he was studying a packet he'd extracted from it. A midnight blue silk robe clung lovingly to his lean, athletic

61

frame, and the bareness of his legs and feet from the knees down suggested that the thin robe was his only protection against the chill of the night.

*Trust you to be prancing about with next to nothing on,* Anna accused him grimly, fighting a losing battle against imagining what lay beneath the lightweight silk. She hugged her own far more substantial robe around her to suppress her own body's instant reaction. Her breasts were tight and sensitized, and deep in the very quick of her belly, desire twisted low, honeyed and traitorous.

Every sense on high alert, she watched Nick place the packet on the counter, and turn his attention, brow still puckered, towards the coffee grinder. One long, elegant hand reached out and fingered the power cord, but then he seemed to think better of it. His lips moved in some unspoken expression of frustration, and he ran his hand through his tousled dark-gold hair.

"It's all right. I'm not going to wake your father up by grinding coffee at this time of night."

The softly spoken words hit Anna like a power-hammer to the chest. How could he know she was here? He couldn't see her from where he was standing, and she could have sworn she hadn't made a sound. But it was too late now to take the soft way out and run.

"I should think not."

Her voice was admirably crisp as she moved into the kitchen and the circle of muted light from the wall lamp, "It's bad enough you creeping around in the small hours like a cat thief without turning on the noisiest appliance in the house into the bargain."

A strange light flared in Nick's blue eyes as he slowly turned towards her. Was it irritation? Arrogant dismissal? Or was it the same betraying desire that she was feeling? It was hard to tell with him. He wore his masks like an Oscar-winning thespian.

"I'm not the only one creeping around," he observed mildly, his glance flicking quickly away from her again, and alighting on the instant-coffee jar. His lusciously modeled mouth quirked with momentary distaste, but he picked up the inferior product nevertheless, then turned his attention to the kettle. "I trust this doesn't whistle to tell us when it's boiling?"

*No, it squawks like a clown's hooter,* she felt like saying, in the hopes it would drive him back to his room, *sans* coffee, in disgust. But instead she said, "No, it's a silent kettle. You needn't worry."

"Good." With no further comment he set about filling the kettle and gathering crockery.

Anna rolled her eyes when he deposited two heaped spoonfuls of coffee granules in one of the mugs, paused, then added another. Typical. When he slanted her a questioning glance, spoon poised over the jar again, she shook her head.

"No. Thanks. I'll make myself some decaffeinated tea if you don't mind." She frowned in the direction of his mug. "How on earth do you expect to get any sleep after drinking a filthy brew like that? You'll be bug-eyed on the ceiling after that lot."

Nick gave a dismissive, very Latin grimace. As the steam rose, he turned and fixed her with a level, almost insolent look.

"Who says I've any intention of sleeping?"

Eyes like twin blue searchlights raked her from her slipper-covered toes to the crown of her disheveled blonde head, and despite her thick, comforting dressing gown and slightly less thick but still comforting nightshirt, Anna shuddered as if she'd been instantly stripped naked.

*Why, oh why didn't I go back to bed when I had the chance?*

63

Fighting the urge not to pull her robe more protectively around her, she settled for fiddling nervously with her sash. When Nick's eyes followed the tiny movement like a bird of prey assessing the strike distance to its victim, she knew she was in big trouble. Yet again.

*Dannazione!* Why did everything about her bother him so much?

Steeling himself not to react, Nick still found himself mesmerized by the compulsive pleating action of Anna's slender fingers as she worried the sash of her voluminous and bizarrely chaste robe.

She had beautiful hands, elegant, smooth-skinned and nimble, and just the mere sight of them had a stunning effect on his body. He suppressed an inner shudder, feeling again the delicate, instinct-guided stroke of those soft fingertips across his aching penis. The way she'd touched him, at first tentatively, then with more confidence.

Ah, *Dio Mio*, how she'd held him.

Groaning inside, he felt that self-same flesh react violently as if crying out for her innocent caress. Summoning a supreme act of self-control, he managed to suppress the most patent evidence of his discomfiture, but even so, he was grateful that once he was sitting at the kitchen table, the cheerful red and white checked cloth masked his groin.

But the heavy atmosphere, latent with a thousand unspoken words and accusations, was more uncomfortable in its own way than his ferocious arousal.

"So?" he queried, unable to bear the electric tension one second longer.

The minute it was out of his lips, he knew he'd miscalculated. About to sit herself, Anna remained on her feet, glaring down at him like an avenging angel swaddled in what looked like twenty layers of night attire. For a moment he thought the cup of tea in her hand was about to end up on his head.

"'So'? What do you mean 'so'? Shouldn't that be my question?"

Her voice was impressively composed, but he could see her knuckles were white. "You pull a fast one on me. You foist your mad scheme on everybody before I've even had an hour or two to digest it, and then you make with the 'so?' as if it's me that's done something wrong."

With enviable self-containment, she sat at the table, facing him, her eyes like a green inferno as she boldly met and held his look.

Another surge of raw, animal feeling wrenched at him.

*Dio*, but she was magnificent.

He'd been with his share of women, all beautiful, all with poise and star quality, all able to make an entrance and dominate a room, play the seductress and captivate a man physically. But Anna possessed a rare quality to which not one of his past girlfriends could hold a candle. An inner spirit and individuality that had haunted him, no matter how he'd tried to deny it. She was a drug in his blood that would never let him rest, always nagging him, always standing between him and the possibility of a wholly satisfying relationship with another woman.

If he didn't get Anna Felgate out of his system somehow, every lover he bedded in the future was doomed to seem ultimately lacking.

"So?" she mocked him, still glaring, her elegant chin up.

Drawing on formidable powers of his own, and the control and self-belief that had always served him admirably in business and with all other women, Nick held his ground. A staring and slanging match was stupid and pointless, so he tried a different angle. Truth—at least partial—and honesty and no more evading critical issues.

"You're right, I made a mistake. I acted in haste and I was unfair to you."

Reaching calmly for his coffee, he took a sip and wrinkled his nose at the less than aromatic taste. "But I was afraid you wouldn't agree to the engagement, and I couldn't risk that, for Carlo's sake. So I moved things on a little more quickly than I should have done."

Anna's brow puckered and she ran her thumb round the rim of her mug, the almost unconscious gesture making Nick feel uncomfortable again.

"Do you think I'd be so cruel and thoughtless that I'd just ignore Carlo's wellbeing?" she challenged, "Of course I want to help. And I know that going along with you is the right thing for the moment." Her eyes narrowed and she gave him a look of sudden, chilly dislike. "But I expected a certain degree of consideration on your part. Assurances. Firmly drawn ground rules."

She set down the mug and Nick noted that she hadn't touched a drop of her tea. "*And* a chance to put Martin in the picture first. He deserves that. If circumstances had been different I might have been announcing my engagement to him tonight. Not you."

He knew she was lying outrageously, but even so, black jealousy enveloped Nick like a descending thunderstorm. The same irrational urge he'd experienced earlier out in the square, the desire to break things, to seek and hunt and obliterate, surged through him. His *sangfroid* teetered on the edge of shattering completely, but by the closest margin he managed to hang on to it. Just.

"I see."

He wanted to roar, but he kept his tone soft. "And an engagement to Johnson is so infinitely more desirable than an engagement to me?" Slowly, with a precision that felt like a Herculean effort, he pushed away his unwanted coffee.

"At least an engagement to Martin would have been genuine. Not the sham that you're suggesting. What happens to Carlo when eventually we have to pretend to call it off again? And what happens to Dad too?" A look of pain flickered across her face, revealing and very real. "He's ecstatic, you know. How's he going to feel when we snatch all this happiness away from him? He's having a hard enough time as it is, what with one thing and another. Don't tell me you don't know that Felgate's is rocky."

*I think I'm in hell.*

Nick was wracked by a turmoil of feelings. For one, he wanted to grab her and shake her over the tales she was telling about her erstwhile boyfriend. Lydia had told him that was going nowhere. For another, he wanted to reach across, take her hand and stroke it gently. He wanted to charge round the accursed table that separated them, envelop her in his arms and tell her everything would be all right and that he would look after both her and her near-bankrupt father for as long as they wanted and needed him. It was a physical pain, the thought she might feel worried or sad or unsure of either her future or her father's. She ought to be safe and secure and cherished forever and ever as long as she lived.

*Maledizione!* What was he thinking? He could never offer her those assurances.

All right, he could take away her father's money worries with the stroke of a pen, something he'd already put measures in place to do, regardless of the success or otherwise of the engagement plan. But those other things? The long-term commitment to one woman, the absolute safety and the cherishing. No. Those he could not offer. It wasn't in his blood.

In a grim flashing moment, he relived the shouting and crying he'd heard as a child, his mother and father arguing with savage bitterness. Those arguments had driven his mother to drink and pills and his father into the arms of other women.

Marriage to a Lisitano man was poisonous, even when there was love there—perhaps especially when there was love there—and it was a deadly chalice that he would never force on any woman. Least of all Anna. To drive her to the tragic end his mother had endured was unthinkable. A death decreed accidental, but which even at a tender age, he'd known in his heart was suicide.

"Nick, are you even listening to me?"

Anna's sudden demand made Nick realize the terrible events of his childhood had taken him away from the problems right at hand.

"Of course," he shot back, the dark memories making his voice harsher than he'd intended, the loss still flooding his mind after all these years. "I trust you'll be tactful and gentle when the time comes. As will I. But my father's recovery right now is my main concern, and I won't allow anything to get in the way of that."

"Not even the fact I'm as good as engaged to another man?"

Again the stubborn lie about Johnson. Caught on the raw, it angered him.

"And yet you responded to me when I kissed you."

His voice remained cool even if inside, his tumultuous

emotions confused and scalded him. Anguish, guilt, long-standing frustrations, all careened around the central, most recent memory, the feel of Anna's velvet-soft lips parting beneath his. The imagined sensation tore at him, and the sexual hunger that had temporarily subsided reasserted itself with gut-twisting intensity.

How dare she go on and on, claiming to care for some insipid boyfriend when she'd participated so uninhibitedly in that kiss? Even now, though there was anger in her eyes, his sexual radar told him she was completely attuned to the incredible chemistry between them.

"You took me by surprise," she replied, the blush of rosy pink across her cheeks undermining her protest. She was holding her poise, just about, but beneath the surface she was whirling in the same maelstrom he was. Anger, confusion, the baggage of the past, the issues of the present...but most of all desire, a force of life that denied all negatives.

*Stop lying! Stop avoiding the issue!*

He didn't know whether it was her he was accusing, or himself. He only knew he wanted her to admit that she wanted *more* than nonentities like Johnson could ever give her. Anna was volcanic and passionate—*Dio*, how he knew that!—and she needed a passionate man with hot red blood in his veins to satisfy her and keep her happy. Granted, he couldn't offer her long-term prospects, the true marriage for both love and sexual compatibility that she really needed. But a brief affair between them, loaded with intense sex and relaxed good times, might exorcise both their respective demons and allow Anna to seek the right long-term relationship eventually.

For her own welfare, he had to break up this ridiculous half-hearted attachment she claimed to have for Martin Johnson, and the sooner he did it, the better.

*Why don't you speak?*

The tension was unbearable. Every drip of the tap, every tick of the clock, every faint traffic sound from the unsleeping metropolis outside seemed to accuse her of being a liar. As did Nick's intense, unwavering blue stare.

What was going on behind those incredible eyes? Why didn't he just accuse her of avoiding the truth? Because heaven knew she *was* avoiding it more desperately than she'd ever avoided anything in her life. She'd responded to Nick because he was still the man she most desired above all men, still the man she should desire least for the sake of the safety of her heart.

*He's not for you. He never will be,* she told herself stringently. *Your body is just stupid and uncontrollable, and it won't listen to reason. You're just letting yourself be beguiled by a beautiful face and the physique of a classical god.*

"I took you by surprise? Oh, I think not, Anna."

His eyes flicked from her face to the way she was fidgeting first with her teacup, then with the tablecloth, then with the sugar tongs. She stilled her hands, realizing she was giving everything away to him so easily.

"You were ready for that kiss," he persisted, a subtle note of triumph coloring his voice. "You were anticipating it. It was *exactly* what you wanted."

"Don't be ludicrous."

Her heart was fluttering. She could feel an arc of high tension building in the air between them. Fighting to hold on to her purpose, she kept her voice steady. "And you're just trying to muddy the issue now too. To distract me with all this BS about kisses, because you *know* you've done something reprehensible and you're trying to bamboozle me into going along with what you want."

She expected him to protest, to claim again that he was only acting in Carlo's interest. Placing her hands on the table, she made to stand, push back her chair and get away from him.

But before she could, he'd leant across the table and put both his bigger, stronger hands over hers, pinning her in place.

"The kiss *is* an issue, Anna." As he came to his feet, he inclined across the table, the cups and the cloth towards her. "It proves that you want me." He paused, his rapier glance settling momentarily on her lips and making them feel as if they'd been licked by fire, "And that I want you."

Anna couldn't move. Theoretically, she could have pulled away, but in every way that mattered, he'd immobilized her. She couldn't look into his eyes—they'd break her apart if she did, crack her right open and reveal her every last secret to him.

But looking at his mouth was worse.

Just to see those sculpted lips was to feel them upon hers. Pressing, bewitching, tasting, controlling. Unconsciously, she licked her own lips in panic, then burnt with shame when he laughed softly and wickedly.

"Stop it!" Managing to break free of his spell at last, she straightened up, almost knocking over her chair. "How can you say you want me? You didn't want me four years ago. Not really. You left me in no doubt whatsoever about that." She edged away, knowing she should run, run like the wind, but still unable to summon the larger action.

Moving with that strange, phenomenal speed of his—the diametric opposite of his customary watchful stillness—Nick shot around the table and in front of her.

She stepped back.

He stepped forward.

She stepped back and back and back until she felt the wall behind her, no retreat. Nick matched every pace until he was so close that she could see the night stubble on his skin, smell his elusive cologne and the faint and even more fugitive odor that was purely and savagely man.

His hands settled on her shoulders, fingertips curling, gripping lightly but unrelentingly.

"It's not that I didn't want you," he murmured low, his breath warm against her temple as he sought to press a single light kiss in her hair. "Never believe that I didn't want you, Anna." Another kiss, even more delicate, on the line of her brow. "It's just that I knew that I shouldn't have had you. Not then. Not like that. You were too young and too trusting."

"That's ridiculous. I was twenty, for God's sake. I've got friends who were married at that age, even with children. And even if I was virgin, I was an adult."

"I shouldn't have taken advantage of you," Nick persisted, steely for a moment, as if she hadn't even spoken.

Anna felt as if she were going to collapse but for Nick's strong hands upon her. "And now?" she heard herself saying, as if from a great distance, "Do you think it's okay to take advantage of me now?"

"Now things are different. It's not taking advantage of you. It's what you need," he growled softly, then brought his mouth down on hers with a singular authority.

*I should shake him off,* she thought faintly, amazed how insubstantial her outrage at his highhandedness felt. *I should wriggle free, get away, do anything but succumb.*

But she couldn't.

Nick's devilish tongue was in her mouth and she was lost, lost, lost. Protest, good sense, self-preservation, everything but the feel, the taste, the power of Nick and his beautiful mouth

72

had as good as vaporized into nothingness. She put up her hands to slide her arms around him and pull him closer, but he prevented it. Instead, his own hands went quickly to work, unfastening her sash, then parting the panels of her robe. With the thick velour out of the way, and just his layer of silk and hers of brushed cotton between them, he pressed the full length of his imperious body against hers and made her know him.

His erection was like a knot of heated stone, jutting against her belly, and she knew that he'd be able to feel hard puckered tips of her breasts against his chest. Pure longing almost made her faint. For four interminable years this was what her body had cried out for, and she gasped and moaned aloud for it now. In a helpless female instinct, she rocked her hips.

Nick laughed deep in his throat, and even though she should have been appalled, and fought him for his profound male arrogance, she couldn't. In fact it only seemed to fuel her flame.

When he freed her mouth her head tipped back against the wall and she moaned again as he dealt swiftly with the buttons at the neck of her nightshirt. Her shoulder bared, he pressed his lips against her naked throat. His tongue, hot and moist, moved delicately over the soft skin there, and once again her pelvis jerked and moved against him.

Long, graceful hands roved over her body, scorching her through the cotton cloth. And when his mouth claimed hers once more, opening her lips with a crushing, confounding pressure, she felt him pluck at the nightshirt and slide it swiftly and deftly upwards.

Her plundered mouth tried vainly to form the word "no"...but it was only going through the motions, an empty gesture. Her heart, her body and soul were screaming "Yes! Yes! Yes!" And that was the cry that Nick was hearing too.

Hot fingertips slid tantalizingly over her bottom and her hip and then spread across her inner thigh, searching, searching...and finding. A heartbeat later, he took possession of the very quick of her.

Still kissing her, still owning her lips and her tongue with his, he began to gently caress the core of her pleasure.

*Nick! Oh Nick!* she cried inside, loving his touch, hungering for it after four years of arid famine.

It didn't take long. Her need was too great, and his skills ineffable. With a ragged whimper into his mouth, she convulsed in climax.

# Chapter Four

"Look, I just don't want to talk about Nick this morning, Lyd. We've got a lot of work to get through and we haven't got time to waste on *him*."

Not to the mention the fact she didn't want to risk her face burning as pink as a peony. Something that happened every time she thought about that scorching encounter last night. It was a sure giveaway, and Lydia would pounce on it.

Every last shred of composure shattered, she'd simply run from the kitchen like a scalded cat when Nick had finally released her from his arms. She'd been too mortified and too confused even to speak, much less make any sense.

How could she have let him touch her like that? And yet, in her heart, and in her still-tingling body, she knew it had been exactly what she'd wanted. What she'd invited, goddamn her libido.

But the truth was still unpalatable. As was her cowardice. Unable to face anybody, she'd been out of the house at the crack of dawn, without breakfast or even coffee.

By six thirty, bleary eyed from less than two hours sleep, and halfway down an early morning Starbucks, she'd been at her desk, sifting through a pile of CVs from prospective applicants. Not that her judgment was really up to it. A serial axe murderer or a porn star could probably have slipped past her at the moment.

And now, unsurprisingly, Lydia was demanding all the dirt from last night. Anna had half expected the older woman to know most of it already, at least the bits that were fit for public consumption, but it seemed that neither Nick nor her father had yet broadcast any word of the engagement.

But why not?

Nick had every reason to make things public immediately, and she couldn't see her father being able to contain the news of his dearest wish come true for very long.

"Something happened. I know it," Lydia persisted, looking disgustingly fresh and unaffected by the amount of champagne she'd consumed the previous evening. "There's still chemistry between the two of you. Even a blind man in blinkers can see that. And chemistry will out, my sweet. Always. Just you believe it," she finished triumphantly.

"That's bullshit, Lyd." Anna strained every nerve to project an airy, unconcerned good humor. "Okay, so Nick's staying at Deverill Square, but that's it. I didn't even see him after the party. And I haven't seen him since."

*Liar, liar, pants on fire!*

She felt a disorientating flush of heat. But not from the lie. Every part of her felt as if it was effervescing—especially those areas that still bore the echo of Nick's touch like a living brand. Even her earlobes were hot. She didn't dare look in the mirror for fear of seeing them actually pulsating.

Her aunt cocked her head on one side, then said, with the delicate sense of tact, "Okay, I can see that whatever it is, you don't want to talk about it just yet."

Anna sighed inwardly, knowing it was only a temporary reprieve.

"But you look exhausted, love," Lydia continued, "Why don't you take a break for a while and I'll make a fresh pot of coffee?"

Oh, bliss. A renewed caffeine hit. Anna smiled gratefully. Lydia was an inveterate gossip and prone to fabricating two and two into seventeen—but she had the most kind and caring heart when it counted.

"That would be divine." Anna slipped into her office chair. "But I'd better crack on with these—" she indicated the CVs, "—so we're ready for the interviews later."

Lydia shrugged and smiled, but left the room, heading for the kitchen. They had an office assistant and a typist who would have gladly made coffee, but Lydia was almost as particular as Nick when it came to its preparation and always insisted on making it herself.

With her aunt busy, Anna sneaked her powder compact out of her bag, and took a peek at the disaster area otherwise known as her face. Even whilst showering, dressing and throwing on a scrap of makeup this morning, she hadn't really been able to look at herself in the eye.

What a monster. She looked ill. Not even a day of facials could have improved matters, so she might as well stick with the light slick of lip-gloss, one coat of mascara, and a little mushroom-colored eye crayon. Her skin was so pallid and washed out that blusher would have made her look like a clown. Beneath her haunted eyes there were delicate lavender shadows.

*This is what you do to me.*

Accusing the absent Nick, she snapped shut her compact and sighed. Scarcely twelve hours had passed since Nick had stepped over the threshold at Deverill Square, and she was already a physical and emotional wreck. How on earth was she going to manage when the real game began?

Mercifully, the morning was busy. Anna interviewed several new prospective temps and was able to sign up two women who fitted the TT profile exactly. The others obviously hadn't read the promotional material at all. Bottom skimming skirts, flimsy tops and heaven forbid, chewing gum, were just not what the agency was looking for.

Lunchtime loomed as Anna exited the small office they used for interviews and found Lydia embroiled in an intense-sounding telephone conversation. One that she terminated abruptly, with the words, "Right, I'll make the arrangements," on catching sight of Anna.

"What's all that about?"

The hairs on the back of Anna's neck popped to attention. There was a shifty look on Lydia's face, and she was fidgeting with her Mont Blanc.

"Good news." The answer was too speedy, and the older woman prodded compulsively at her collapsing chignon. "A mid-sized manufacturing company called Deighton Industries has just been taken over, and their London operation is undergoing a shake-up. They're looking for lots of clerical staff on short-term contracts, especially PAs for some of their execs. That was their new...um...Human Resources guy on the phone. He'd like to meet one of us straight away to set something up."

"Right now?" Anna was used to high-powered business executives wanting premium staff at a click of their well-manicured fingers, but straight away was shorter notice than was usual.

"Yes. Over a working lunch, at their offices in Maybury Street. It's not far away. If you get a taxi you can be there in a few minutes."

"Me? But you're the one he's spoken to. Won't he be expecting you?" Anna narrowed her eyes. Lydia was looking more and more uneasy by the minute.

"I said it would be you. I...I'm not feeling too hot, Anna. Last night's champagne, you know." Lydia gave her an almost pleading look, rubbing her ample middle for effect.

"Okay. I'll go."

Anna felt a strange fluttering sensation in her own stomach all of a sudden. Not from champagne—she'd barely drunk any— but from lack of sleep, appalling emotional tension and an uneasy gut feeling of disquiet.

"Attagirl, Anna. It's a huge opportunity for us. It could lead to long-term contracts too. Really set us up."

*Yes, we do need this*, thought Anna, *and as many other deals like it as we can get. If we're to justify me refusing a funding offer from Nick we've got to snatch every opportunity that comes our way.*

Around twenty minutes later, Anna was staring at a depressingly bland print hanging in the foyer at Deighton Industries. The overly made-up receptionist had gestured to a long sofa against the wall, explaining that someone would be down to meet her in a moment, but Anna felt too edgy to relax. This was an important meeting, but it was more than that. Her over-taxed ESP was pinging with warning messages.

At the sound of lift doors opening, it was an effort to turn around. And when she did, why was it not the slightest surprise to see who was walking towards her?

"Welcome to Deighton Industries, Miss Felgate," said Nick, an impossibly smug expression on his golden face as he extended his hand for an innocuous businessman's greeting. "I'm so glad you could spare me some time. Won't you come this way?" A heartbeat later he was beside her, long, determined fingers planted squarely in the small of her back to guide her towards the claustrophobic cage of the lift compartment.

"Thank you, *Signor* Lisitano, I can manage," she shot back, darting ahead to escape the incendiary pressure of his fingertips. Clean through her clothes, they felt like firecrackers against her skin. Heat migrated through her body with a terrifying speed and settled in all the zones that were still reacting to the night before.

As the lift doors enclosed them, she turned on him.

"If you'd wanted to speak to me, Nick, you could just have called. I'm sure Lydia's given you my number." She faced him boldly, because it was no good cowering and hiding. She couldn't undo what was done—she just had to live with it.

"And would you have answered?"

His illuminated sapphire eyes steady and challenging, Nick leant back against the lift compartment's wall and shoved his hands into his trouser pockets. He was wearing another superb suit today, a dark business three piece with a dazzling white shirt that turned his Mediterranean tan molten. In contrast to the tousled curliness of last night, his amazing hair was faultlessly groomed, every gleaming strand combed back neatly from his smooth, broad brow line.

He was a corporate god, charming, urbane, immaculate— and totally unstoppable.

"Anna?" he prompted, and to her horror, Anna realized she'd just been standing there ogling him. Drinking him in like a draught of crystal water in a desert.

"No...probably not. I...I needed a bit of breathing space from you."

And she needed it now. More than ever. The lift compartment was minute and the scent of Nick's cologne and the lingering imprint of his fingertips on her back were doing abominable things to her composure.

"Just as I thought," he remarked as the lift shuddered to halt and mercifully the doors slid open, "So I was obliged to take measures." He made a swift gesture, clearly with the intention of settling his guiding hand on her back once more, but Anna shot ahead like a rabbit from a trap, cursing at herself.

When would she ever learn it was fatal to let Nick know he was getting to her?

"So as usual you use sneaky tricks to get what you want," she snipped back, stomping into the middle of the office he'd directed her towards. It was a pleasant enough room, but as characterless as the foyer. Nothing like the standard of luxury Nick was accustomed to.

"Because you drive me to them."

His voice pointed, Nick came around to face her and they stood like a pair of pugilists about to knock seven bells out of each other.

Suppressing all reaction, Anna opened her mouth, but he forestalled her, a smile of total, glorious confidence on his face. Oh, why oh why was he so unfeasibly good looking?

"But your presence here is legitimate, *cara mia.*" Cocking his shining head on one side, he looked her up and down with the unique combination of insolence and raw sexual admiration of which only a testosterone-drenched Italian male was capable. "The takeover here has created an increased workload. More bodies are needed and Traditional Temps is the ideal choice to supply some of the key personnel."

Anna pursed her lips. He was one of the world's most consummate dissemblers, yet he could be telling the truth, at least partially. "Well, I'm delighted you're considering us, but don't you have people of your own to do your hiring? I mean, it isn't usually the CEO of a company who sees to the setting on of a few extra secretaries, is it?"

The slow, assessing smile widened. "Well, you know me, Anna. I've always been a hands-on kind of guy." Impossibly thick lashes swept down for just a second, and then his blue gaze swept down her body and lingered around hip level with burning emphasis.

Anna stifled a gasp as if she'd taken a blow to the solar plexus. Confused emotions tumbled through her like an avalanche. Burning embarrassment. Consuming anger. A heavy, shaming twist of stark, unadulterated desire. She began to blush again and her knees felt as if they were about to liquefy. In an instinctive gesture of protection, she swung her laptop case around in front of her body.

"What's that?" Nick enquired, tracking the action, "A makeshift chastity belt?" He was still smiling, still devastating her. "I'm hardly likely to attempt to touch you right here in this office, am I? Someone will be here any moment with our lunch."

Anna let the case slip to her side, and straightened her spine. No! He was not going to get the better of her this time, either verbally or otherwise.

"Can we please discuss your staffing situation then? I'm sure a busy man like you has only a limited amount of time to spare, and for my part, the sooner we've covered the ground and I can go the better." She met his blue gaze unflinchingly and assumed a neutral smile, "I do have a number of other clients to see this afternoon."

"And you'll be able to deal with them much more efficiently with lunch inside you. Come and sit." One long, narrow-fingered hand gestured to an informal seating area at the far end of the room, where two mud-colored, but reasonably comfortable looking sofas were set right angles to each other around a low, square coffee table. "Lydia tells me you were in the office at the crack of dawn this morning, which I suspect means you didn't eat a proper breakfast."

There was no way she was going to tell him he was right on the money.

"Thank you for your concern, Nick, but it's unnecessary," she countered, attempting to project serenity and an air of being completely unruffled by his underhand tactics. "But I had a perfectly good breakfast, so don't worry."

"But an early one," he pointed out, and when it looked as if he was going to take her by the arm and drag her to the seating area by main force, Anna walked smoothly across the room under her own steam. Nick followed her and—an outrageous chauvinist with perfect manners—he remained standing until she took her seat.

With exaggerated care, Anna placed her shoulder bag and her laptop case alongside her, attempting to fill the entire sofa, but with a quirk of his eyebrow, Nick picked up both bags again and set them aside. In a smooth, fluid, totally relaxed movement, he settled himself beside her, long legs crossed, his thigh inches from hers.

*So it's like this, is it?* Anna sighed inwardly, attempting to neutralize responses that were firing helplessly in his proximity. Her body was at Condition Red, inner klaxons screaming. "May I have my case back, please," she said, feigning a quiet, businesslike demeanor. "I need it for my presentation."

"There's no need for a presentation."

Nick leant back against the upholstery, one arm draping casually along the sofa back behind her. "I made all the arrangements with Lydia on the phone. It's a done deal."

This time Anna did sigh. She couldn't help herself. There

was no way to win with this man. He always got his own way, and he seemed to have fewer scruples about it now than he'd ever had.

Smoothing her hands down the slim, dark grey skirt of her suit, she prepared to rise. "Well, I'll be on my way then. Enjoy your sandwiches, Nick."

A perfectly calibrated grip fastened around her wrist and strong yet gentle, he kept her in her seat.

"We need to talk, Anna. We need to have the conversation we should have had last night, before...well...before things got out of hand." His blue eyes flashed, darkening suddenly, and Anna found herself trembling, her mind and heart and body transported back to the kitchen, back to the wall, and back to the consciousness-warping sensations of Nick's assured, exploring touch. She looked away, filled with embarrassment, wanting to be both a million miles away from him and yet there again, writhing as his fingers worked their magic.

What was to become of her? How could she ever go through with this scheme of Nick's when she went up in flames every time he touched her? Why couldn't she detach herself and act like a mature, pragmatic grown-up instead of the infatuated, lust-crazed little tart she'd been four years ago when she'd been so desperate to lose her virginity to him.

But she knew the reason, and as she forced herself to look into Nick's burning eyes again, her heart turned over at the enormity of the revelation.

Yes, she'd been sexually inexperienced four years ago, but she hadn't been infatuated or lust-crazed. She'd simply been in love with him.

As she still was.

Nick watched a tapestry of emotions weave itself across the

smooth porcelain contours of Anna's face. She looked as if she'd just been felled by a terrible shock and had the bottom of her world kicked out from under her. He longed to hold her close and rock and comfort her in his arms.

He couldn't bear the thought of anyone hurting her, but knew that his out-of-control actions of last night had probably done just that.

Not at the time though. She'd been right there with him, his passionate match, her magnificent erotic spirit rising exquisitely to his touch. But in the aftermath, when she'd flown the room, he'd realized to his chagrin that he'd taken far too much from her far too soon. Again.

*What the hell is the matter with me?* Shame at his own sexual greed washed through him. With any other woman I'd have been far subtler and more circumspect.

"Are you all right, Anna?"

Self-disgust made his voice sound far harsher than he'd intended. "You've gone as white as milk."

"It's nothing. I'm all right." Visibly pulling herself together, she straightened and tried to free herself from the grip he suddenly realized he was exerting on her. He released her instantly, then watched her rub at her wrist.

*Per Dio*, had he hurt her physically too now?

"It is rather a long time since breakfast," she conceded, "Maybe I'll have one of those sandwiches after all."

"Excellent, I'll see where they are." Starting to rise, it was his turn to feel himself restrained. Boldly, she'd caught hold of his wrist, and it felt like the charge from an electric cattle prod had shot clean through his body. He only prayed his wayward cock wouldn't react too obviously. It had a habit of betraying him whenever he got too near to her.

"No rush." As she released him he experienced an immediate pang of untenable loss. It had only been his wrist, yet the contact had been heavenly. "We do need to talk, Nick. You're right," she offered, her voice hesitant as if talking to him was the last thing she wanted to do.

Oh, now she was prepared to talk?

Nick felt a rush of illogical irritation. He'd been the one who'd forced this conversation, but faced with it, he suddenly wished they could avoid it.

Why couldn't they have a pleasant, companionable lunch instead? Just be friends and get to know one another properly again? He suddenly realized he craved that just as much as he desired her beautiful, lithe body. Perhaps even more...

But she did look beautiful.

Anna was so full of surprises, of new variations, each one delighting him in a different way to the last. He thought of the flirty little dress she'd worn at the party—that had suggested rather than revealed her shape in a way that had been both elegant and provocative.

Then there had been that shapeless feed sack of a dressing gown, which against all reason had still turned him on with thoughts of what was so voluminously concealed beneath it.

And now, here she was in this sober but feminine little suit, its slim dark grey skirt just brushing her delectable knees. He loved the way the neat white shirt she wore with it seemed to highlight the faultless beauty of her face and the elfin perfection of her short golden hair.

Anna frowned, and Nick realized he must have been staring at her, with a no doubt inappropriate expression of male sexual appraisal on his face.

*She's driving me mad*, he thought, feeling a rare moment of confused despair. *Why does this always happen?*

With other women, even in the most intense relationships, even in the steamiest, most rampant encounters in bed, he could always maintain a measure of detachment, of control. But with Anna, he was totally connected, all the time, every bit of him centered on her.

*So. Talk. Yes.* Per Dio, *let's get on with it.*

And as he marshaled the facts of their situation, applying all the logic he could, one monumental issue immediately reared its head. One he suspected Anna really wanted to gloss over, get around, and generally pretend didn't exist. Well, she was going to have to face it. Right now. And so was he.

"So, *cara*," he began, relaxing back more comfortably on the sofa, fixing his eyes on hers, "When you explain to your boyfriend about our engagement, will you mention what happened last night in the kitchen?"

It hit her so hard she appeared to almost physically reel, and remorse struck Nick a reciprocal blow.

He'd done it again, just moments after resolving to behave himself. Surely he could have been more delicate? More considerate? It seemed not. When he was around her he just charged ahead regardless like some hormone-crazed Neanderthal.

But how could he not be aroused? Her heart-shaped face was flushed with the most tantalizing wild roses, the glow so very similar to the hectic color brought on by orgasm. And her huge green eyes were as brilliant as they were in the throes of sex. She was even breathing hard, just as she'd done when his body had been pressed against hers last night.

"Last night was a hideous mistake. It shouldn't have happened. You've got to forget it." Her voice was low, gritty with intent.

"Aren't those supposed to be my lines?" Nick cut back,

caught on the edge not only by the awful irony of her words, but also by the intense sensuality of her brightly fevered appearance.

"Maybe so, but it's my turn to speak them now. Because that's how I feel."

Nick shook inside. He could feel a whirlwind fighting to rise inside him. The same volatile lack of sense, control and moderation that in his father had created a living hell for his mother. He tamped it down ruthlessly.

"Well, I don't regret what I did," he commented more coolly, surprised and pleased that he hadn't lost it. "Touching you was beautiful to me, *tesoro mio*. And I had hoped you found some beauty in it too."

Anna's face was a picture of confusion. Of disorderly emotions. She *had* been there with him! She *had*. The urge to sweep her back into his arms and do the same again, and much, much more, was like agony in his blood. But just as before, he controlled the desire with the sternest efficiency.

"I...I was tired, Nick. I wasn't thinking straight. And sometimes you can just be...well...a bit overwhelming."

"So, all my fault then?" he observed, still gripped by the craziness and emotions that were probably just as unstable as hers, washing around inside him.

"Yes. No. Oh, I don't know!" Her voice was ragged, and Nick was back to guilt again, harsh, grinding guilt. What the hell was it about her that made him act like such a complete fool?

Taking a calming breath, he leant forward and gently took her hand. He felt her flinch, but she didn't pull back, even though she had every right to be skittish around him. "Look, let's take time out. Not apportion blame. Just accept."

She nodded, pursed her lips, seemed to compose herself even though he could still feel a fine trembling in her fingers.

"We are attracted to each other, you must admit that." He kept his tone steady and rational. "And in some circumstances, and situations, it tends to get the better of us."

He flashed her a questioning look, wondering if she'd concede that, then saw her nod again. "But from now on, I'll do my best to contain myself rather than make things awkward for you." He patted the hand he was holding with his other one, "Although if you want me to do otherwise, please tell me, won't you? I wouldn't like to think I was holding back when you wanted to be in my arms."

Extricating her hand from his, Anna gave a sudden, soft laugh and her body seemed to finally relax. "Good God, Nick, you really are the living end, you know." A wry smile illuminated her face. "You actually believe that you're completely irresistible, don't you?"

*Do you really, really want to resist me?* he longed to say, but prudence and a need to preserve this lighter mood stayed his tongue. "One tries, *bella mia*," he demurred, smiling back at her, "One tries."

She shook her head as if in despair and seemed just about to say something else when there was a knock at the door that stole away the fugitive words.

"Come!" called Nick, and the door opened to reveal the personal aide who'd been temporarily assigned to him by the Deighton management. She bore a large tray holding their lunch.

A few moments selecting sandwiches and pouring coffee provided a welcome respite, but pretty soon Nick could see that Anna's appetite for food was as insubstantial as his. She took a microscopic bite of a sandwich, then put her plate aside, looking ill at ease again. Her fingers flexed, as if about to reach for her coffee, but then she took a deep breath and appeared to brace herself to face some thorny difficulty or pitfall.

"I'll have to talk to Martin as soon as possible. This can't go any further without him knowing. It's not fair."

Picking up a paper napkin to wipe her fingers, she began to shred it compulsively, and Nick wondered if she even knew that she was doing it. "I...I should have phoned him this morning," she admitted, finally looking down at the mess of white fragments in her hand and hastily dropping them on her plate, "But...I was distracted. As you can well imagine." As she finished, her head came up and her eyes met his defiantly.

"Indeed."

Setting aside his own unwanted food, Nick strove to conceal his gathering sense of triumph. Once again, he'd managed to expunge the Englishman from Anna's thoughts and emotions. It was only a matter of time before she realized men like Johnson would never satisfy her.

"I'll call him when I get back to the office. Invite him around this evening. Maybe cook him a meal and explain everything to him." The tension around her soft pink mouth told Nick that this wasn't a prospect she relished.

All the better that she didn't have to face it alone.

"That won't be necessary. I've made all the arrangements. No need to worry."

"What do you mean? What *arrangements*?"

Anna was frowning, her eyes stormy again, but for a second all Nick could think about was the old cliché about a woman looking beautiful when she was angry. There was an avenging war goddess just inches away from him and the urge to fall down and worship her was so strong that his limbs tensed, ready for action.

"I've booked a table for the three of us this evening at La

Girandole. Eight thirty. I thought it would be more pleasant to discuss our 'situation' in relaxed surroundings and over good meal."

"The *three* of us? Are you out of your mind?"

Anna threw back her head and stared at the ceiling. She looked tenser and more aggravated than ever, but the sensuous line of her elegant white throat was suddenly all that Nick could focus on. The sweet taste of her skin was in his mouth again and the texture of it fiery against his lips. He wanted to kiss, lick, explore—maybe even nip at her with his teeth until she moaned with desire.

"I'm *not* telling Martin about all this with you there. It's going to be hard enough as it is. What on earth are you thinking about? It's insane."

*I'm thinking about kissing your neck, amore mio,* Nick told her silently, but instead he observed. "I thought my presence would make things easier for you. Johnson is hardly likely to behave unpleasantly if I'm there to support you, is he?"

For the most fleeting of moments, he saw relief cross her face and it sluiced through him too, like an invigorating shower. Yes. In her subconscious at least she was already aligned with him rather than with that insipid nonentity Johnson.

"What do you mean 'behave unpleasantly'? Martin isn't like that. He's sensible and reasonable. A perfect gentleman." She flashed him a savage, cutting look. "Not like some people I could mention."

"Sensible? Reasonable? A perfect gentleman? What a thrilling sex life you two must have."

Anna was on her feet in half a heartbeat, and Nick wanted to kick himself. He'd done it yet again. Upset her like some jealous adolescent. Why had he no control over himself whatsoever where the question of Anna's relationships with other men was concerned?

"I'm sorry! I'm sorry."

Up just as quickly, he clasped her arm and prevented from leaving as she so obviously intended to, "Can't you see I'm simply envious of his right to be with you?"

And never more than now.

Anna's breasts were heaving and her eyes were flashing sparks like a blade against steel. He imagined pulling her to him, crushing his mouth against hers as he ground his sudden, fierce hardness against her exquisite softness.

"Let me go, Nick." Her voice was low and deadly. She meant business. He released her arm, but the thought of her walking out cut him to the quick.

Amazingly, she stayed.

Her voice was astonishingly calm as she spoke. "Look, I want to help Carlo. You know I care for him. But if you don't stop sniping at Martin and making things impossible for me...I...I don't know how I can go through with this thing."

The thought of his father brought a blessed clarity to Nick's thoughts.

"You're right, of course. I'm behaving like a fool. It won't happen again."

Anna glanced about, distracted, looking as if she'd almost hoped that he might do something drastic.

"All right. Okay...but I don't think this dinner is such a good idea," she responded quickly, her body full of tension and an obvious desire to get away from him as soon as possible. The urge to curse himself, volubly and savagely in his own tongue, grew stronger than ever.

"Perhaps not," he conceded, shrugging and wondering how she would take what he had to tell her next, "But your boyfriend has already agreed to it. He's going to meet us at the restaurant, at the appointed time."

Anna's mouth dropped open, and Nick could see that his latest *fait accompli* had completely sideswiped her. Just as it had done very much the same when he'd spoken to Johnson on the phone earlier.

He recalled the Englishman's surprise and mystification at being invited to dinner with his own girlfriend by another man. At first he'd blustered a little, but when Nick had subtly hinted there might be certainly high-paying contacts that might be put the way of Johnson's law firm, he'd reluctantly capitulated.

*Too easy*, thought Nick, his mouth twisting in momentary disgust. In Johnson's place, he would have been round here without drawing a breath, demanding the full story, surging like a knight errant defending his lady. In Johnson's place he would have categorically refused to allow another man to drive his girlfriend to the restaurant. Possibly emphasizing his point with the threat of physical violence.

"Martin agreed to it?" Anna queried, her smooth brow puckering in disbelief.

"Yes, he seemed to think it would be an excellent idea," lied Nick, resisting the urge to point out that if she'd cared about the man at all she would have phoned him by now and be fully aware of what was going on.

"Does he know what you want to meet him for?"

"No, not precisely. I simply told him I had a proposal to discuss with him." Nick studied her face, watching her every perplexed reaction. "I didn't specify what type of proposal I had in mind."

"I still think it would be better to meet at Deverill Square." She pursed her lips, clearly thinking hard. "Like I said, there's no danger of Martin making a fuss. He's a solicitor. He's used to

93

difficult negotiations."

"And so am I, if you recall. As my father's troubleshooter it's my business." Nick clasped his hands and studied the knuckles of his left hand. "But if he should choose to criticize you for your decision to help me, I might have to take issue with that," he finished with emphasis.

Anna's eyes flared like green fire. "You're not seriously suggesting that you'd hit him if you don't get your own way? For heaven's sake, Nick, grow up."

"Of course not. What sort of barbarian do you think I am?" Nick replied coolly, although not without wondering exactly how he would feel if anyone were to hurt Anna in any way. It would be untenable. "But I *am* Italian, and we're a volatile race. I can't guarantee that I wouldn't lose my temper." For a brief second, he thought with bitterness of his parents' marital rages.

Anna let out a heavy sigh and put a long, slender hand to her face. She seemed almost oblivious to her own action, but it made Nick experience a poignant twist of longing.

Oh, to feel her touching *his* face, stroking it with tenderness, with desire.

The shrill bell-like ringtone of his mobile phone shattered his moment of silent yearning. Inwardly cursing, he plucked the unit from his pocket and flipped it open, intending to cancel the call without answering.

"*No! Non ora!*" The words slipped out harshly when he saw the number displayed in the tiny back-lit panel, probably the very last one he wanted to connect to right at this moment.

Please not now, he thought, pressing OK with a sense of heavy trepidation.

# Chapter Five

Watching the square outside, Anna wondered yet again why she'd agreed to this three-way dinner. It seemed predoomed to turn into a disaster, yet somehow he'd made it sound like a rational, civilized way to go about things. At the time.

Now, she was dreading it. Letting out a sigh, she rubbed her temple in small circles with her fingertips.

Great. The evening hadn't even begun and she already had a headache gathering. No real surprise there though. Emotional tension almost always triggered her occasional migraines—and in the last twenty-four hours she'd probably had more of that than in her entire life to date. And ninety-nine per cent of it could be laid squarely at Nick's door.

It was Nick who had forced himself into centre stage of her life when for four years she'd managed to banish him to the periphery.

It was Nick whose pre-emptive strike had put her in the ludicrous situation of being engaged to him when she should have been getting engaged, if not to Martin, then to somebody sensible like him.

It was Nick who, virtually without effort, had roused the sleeping demon of her mindless sexual desire for him and put her entire emotional wellbeing in deadly peril.

"I'd hate you if I didn't love you," she growled as she strode yet again to the window to look out for him. Not that she couldn't manage both at once.

For some reason best known to himself, Nick hadn't returned to stay at Deverill Square after last night's debacle. Anna presumed that he was back at the Savoy. Wouldn't want to be too far from your fabulous designer wardrobe, would you, Signor Fashion Victim? What sartorial ensemble would he materialize in tonight, she wondered? Something exceptional and high-end, but undoubtedly understated. Even though he was a beautiful dresser he was anything but flashy.

She grimaced. Poor Martin dressed quite well too, but he just didn't have high style in his blood that even the humblest Italian male did. Nor did he have the limitless assets of a billionaire playboy.

A circuit of the room, then back to the window again, and still no sign of Nick.

Anna shuddered, her thoughts returning to Martin.

Their recent phone conversation had been prickly. Never one to discuss feelings, Martin had sounded stilted, and uncharacteristically befuddled, and he'd completely avoided the deeper implications of Nick's request for a meeting. His main concern seemed to be what his mother would think about Anna being seen with another man.

"It's a bit irregular, Anna," he'd said, "You know Mother is a stickler about that sort of thing."

*What sort of thing?* Anna wanted to ask. *Since when have we been living in the Victorian age?*

But instead, she'd kept her cool and said, "Well, perhaps you should have insisted on picking me up yourself and taking me to La Girandole? I'm sure Nick wouldn't have minded."

Hesitation. "Well, he seemed quite firm that he pick you

up," Martin demurred, a cross edge in his voice. "And it doesn't do to alienate rich and powerful men, does it? A person like that has a lot of influence."

*He certainly does,* she thought, a sinking, shifting feeling attacking her middle, bringing with it a sense of resentment. Partly against Nick, for thinking he could play people games just because he'd set his mind on something and because he *was* rich and powerful. But more than that, she felt irritated with Martin for not standing up to him. And for not expressing the slightest hint of jealousy. If the tables had been turned, Nick wouldn't have stood for his own high-handed actions.

Was Martin really the one she'd ever wanted to be with? *Instead* of Nick? She supposed she'd turned a blind eye to a man in his thirties' habit of constantly deferring to his mother. And that slight hint of acquisitiveness. Being fairly easy-going, she'd not let it get to her. Until now, when faced with an entirely different kind of questionable male behavior from another quarter.

Mulling things over, her attention was wrenched away from inner debate by the entirely unexpected phenomenon of someone speaking Nick's name *on the television.*

Anna had been watching the box on and off while she'd been waiting. Although her father constantly teased her about it, one of her favorite shows was an early evening magazine called Paparazzi Beat. It was hilariously trashy, covering the lives and loves of the rich and famous, and celebrities, pseudo and otherwise in the most lurid terms. Anna watched it, she supposed in her heart of hearts, for the same reason she devoured the celebrity magazines.

Because every now and there was news of Nick and his latest female conquest.

This news-byte was half over by the time she focused in on

it, but her heart leapt into her throat at the sight of the notoriously temperamental film star Maria Rossi looking characteristically distraught as she left the set of the film she was making in London. Her eyes covered by huge shades, and her red lips clamped in a sullen line, she was clinging—like a limpet—to a very familiar escort.

Oblivious to the chattering presenter, Anna glared at the solicitous way Nick handed the Italian beauty into her car and the perfect match the two of them made together. Both were elegant and breath-catchingly attractive, and figures of such intrinsic glamour that they seemed on a different plane to the mere mortals who observed them.

Then, suddenly, something dawned on Anna. Almost grabbed her by the throat.

The clip was either live or very recently recorded because Nick was wearing exactly the same dark, exquisitely tailored three-piece business suit he'd had on at lunchtime. Teamed with exactly the same white shirt and subtle but distinctively patterned tie.

"So *that's* who phoned you."

Anna frowned at the screen, even though the presenter had moved on to another story. "She's the one you as good as dismissed me like a minion for, and couldn't get out of the room fast enough for."

She was exaggerating, of course. Nick had expressed genuine regret at having to curtail their impromptu business lunch, and the expression on his face when he'd given her a peck on the cheek at their parting had been most peculiar. But now, glancing down at the sexy little dark mauve vintage top and sleek black trousers she'd chosen for the evening, and her favorite pair of strappy heels, Anna wondered whether it had been worth all the agonizing over her appearance for tonight.

Nick was no doubt with his Italian film goddess now. His *real* girlfriend.

His fake fiancée would be the last thing on his mind.

*I can't do this.*

Anna paced a bit, hugging herself and trying to ease the grim sensation in her heart. Images of Nick and Maria poured into her mind like acid. There was no way she could put on the act he wanted her to, smiling and behaving as if she adored him, and he her.

Not when his nights were spent naked in the arms of one of the most beautiful women in the entire world.

Expecting a phone call any moment to say the dinner was off, Anna flinched in astonishment when, a short while later, she saw a low, black aerodynamic shape come gliding into the square. Irrational excitement and hope accompanied the thrumming, throaty, growling roar that seemed to shake the very glass she was peering through.

Nick had come to collect her in his Lisitano Vampiro.

The moment the car slid to a halt, Anna sprang back from the window. No way must he know she'd been looking out for him like dopey emo teenager pining for her boyfriend. Even if that was more or less what she *had* been doing. Snapping off the offending television, she wished to heaven that she'd never turned it on in the first place.

Now it was impossible to indulge in her secret little deluded fantasies that Nick actually cared for her in the way she'd once dreamed of, as well as needing her for his schemes. Last night's kisses—and the touching—hadn't been about genuine desire for *her* but simply a red-blooded male seizing the moment, and a bit of sexual titillation with a woefully needy woman whose backbone resembled that of a jellyfish.

Yet, despite the sobering realizations, when the doorbell trilled, mad fluttering butterflies took flight in her chest.

*Dear heaven, I'm actually looking forward to this,* she thought, trying to hold on to her deep breathing exercises. *I've missed the bastard. And only since lunchtime. I'm insane.*

For four years, she'd barely seen Nick Lisitano at all and done her best not to even think about him—yet now, after only a few hours, she felt pain if he wasn't in the vicinity.

Why on earth had she let things get this bad, this soon? She didn't *want* to feel this way. She'd believed she'd inoculated herself against Nick forever. But now it would have been easier not to breathe than to stop yearning for him.

The bell trilled again and she swung open the door.

"Good evening, Anna. Have you missed me?"

Nick's voice was light, and his blue eyes teased her as he stood on the doorstep, hands in his pockets, his stance totally relaxed yet vaguely challenging.

He'd changed out of the buttoned-up business suit that Maria Rossi had been fawning all over, and the one he wore now was more casual and less structured, but still sublime. It's muted, grey-blue color, along with the darker tones of his matching shirt and tie, brought out the brilliance of his eyes with enormous drama, and its fluid styling suggested the raw athleticism of the body beneath the cloth.

He looked amazing, as ever. And as ever, he was completely aware of the fact.

"No, not at all," lied Anna smoothly, intensely satisfied when Nick's brow puckered. "In fact, I'm surprised you even bothered to turn up at all."

"Why would you say that?"

He sounded perplexed and a little angry, and suddenly

Anna couldn't blame him. Her greeting had been less than gracious and it made her feel decidedly bratty in hindsight.

"I didn't mean to, actually," she backtracked, then paused to check her bag for her keys, her purse and her handkerchief. It was a displacement activity to avoid looking Nick in the eye. "It's just been a busy day and I'm a bit tired. Take no notice of me. Shall we go?"

The sooner they got started, the sooner this potential disaster would be over. Snatching up the pashmina she'd draped over the hall chair, she flashed him a tight, plastic grin.

"I thought I might come in and say good evening to Clive." Nick's sharp gaze scanned her, a hint of worry in his sculpted features. Without warning, he reached out and softly cupped Anna's cheek, making her shiver involuntarily, "If you're not well, *cara*, we don't have to go out."

"I'm fine. Really. We need to get this over with, don't we? And Martin's waiting." Anna wished Nick would take his fingers away. They were doing shocking and disturbing things to her entire system. Weak with instant desire, she had to consciously stop herself leaning into the pressure of his touch and purring with the pleasure of it.

Nick frowned again, and his long hand flexed momentarily before withdrawing. "Okay. If you're sure? But perhaps we can just spare a moment to say hello to your father?"

"I'm afraid he's gone out to dinner with Lydia and a group of friends. It's a belated birthday thing for some people who couldn't be here last night."

At that, Nick simply nodded and gestured towards the car. "Let's go then, shall we?"

Confronted by the crouching, menacing vehicle, Anna thanked the stars she'd chosen to wear trousers. Even so, getting into the low, streamlined cockpit was going to be a stiff test in not looking like a total klutz. In a skirt she would have had to flash a long expanse of thigh—and perhaps more—and after last night she wasn't prepared to gift Nick with an opportunist sighting of her knickers.

Surprisingly though, when Nick popped the dramatic gull-wing passenger door, Anna managed to slither into the car with a nice bit of grace, helped by the clasp of his supporting hand. The glint in his eye, however, when his gaze traveled the whole length of her legs, told her he'd been aware of her qualms about underwear, skirts and cars.

She got another pleasant surprise when Nick thumbed the ignition button. Expecting a deafening ten-cylinder engine roar, the sound filtering through into the luxurious vehicle from under the bonnet was little more than a gentle rumble.

The deceptively casual tone of Nick's voice was infinitely more intimidating than any amount of high revs.

"So, why did you think I might not turn up?"

*Because I saw you with that woman, and she was draped all over you like a second skin, and I was so jealous I wanted to scratch her eyes out.*

For a moment, Anna had a hideous feeling she'd spoken out loud, but in the face of Nick's continued, pressuring silence, it seemed she hadn't.

"I saw you on the television," she blurted out at last, "You were with Maria Rossi, and you were getting into a car together...and it was today."

Nick's gear change was as smooth as silk, but there was underlying aggression.

"Yes, I saw Maria today." The words were cool and throwaway, as if escorting one of the world's most beautiful women was nothing unusual, "But that's no reason to believe I wouldn't keep my date with you. Surely you know that I'd have contacted you if there were a problem?"

Why did Nick always have the knack of making her feel as if she were an envious, nagging harpy? And why had he called this evening a *date*, when that was the last thing it was?

"Yes, I do know that," she conceded, feeling the inner brat surge up again and disliking her intensely. "But you and she looked awfully...um...friendly. I...I thought you might want to be together tonight."

Nick flashed her a fleeting glance out of the corner of his eye, without losing one iota of his concentration on the road. "Are my ears deceiving me? It sounds to me as if you're jealous, *cara*," he said softly.

*Of course I am!*

She wanted to rage at him, but that would only induce another of those arrogant, sexy smiles of his. The ones so infuriating that she was driven to thoughts of petty violence sometimes.

All men liked to imagine scores of women were vying jealously for their attention, and Nick was clearly no exception.

Again came that sudden inner flash. The vision of Nick in bed with Maria, the two of them making love, their bodies matched and mated. It was all Anna could do not to groan out loud.

But instead, she summoned a monumental effort of composure. "Of course I'm not jealous," she fibbed lightly, "I have Martin. You have Maria...and any others you've got on the go at the moment."

Nick said nothing, but she could still hear that laugh of his. Low, husky and mocking. He knew she *was* jealous. She was giving herself away with everything she said and everything she did, despite her best efforts not to.

As the silence between them stretched on and on, the urge to fill it seemed to grow like a gathering weight. Anna decided she simply had to speak, even if it meant giving herself away again.

"This is a fabulous car. I heard tell that you had some input into the design?" Her voice sounded unnaturally bright in the enclosed space.

"A little only. AL has a superb design team. They don't need the boss's son interfering, but they're all tactful enough to listen to my suggestions."

But it wasn't just tact. For all their differences, Anna couldn't deny that Nick was a Renaissance man. He had an awesome business brain, and yet he had the soul of an artist and an adventurer too. In addition to his design skills, he'd actually driven for Automotivo Lisitano in competition, in touring cars and even briefly in F1. He'd never won a race, as he'd never been able to commit completely to the sport, but he'd always acquitted himself with daring and panache and had once even been on the podium.

She glanced at those beautiful hands resting so lightly yet commandingly on the steering wheel and imagined them wrestling with the controls of a much more volatile race car. He was so strong, so deft, so sure of himself. In all things.

Suddenly the car's cockpit closed in on her like a movie special effect. The sounds, the scents and the sensations grew almost touchable. She fancied she could feel the air move against her skin as Nick changed gear again, and the waft of it brought the smell of his spicy cologne to her nostrils. The unique scent of him intoxicated her, blended as it was with the expensive aroma of fine leather upholstery and the fugitive machine tang of the powerful engine block.

Beneath the automotive music of the Vampiro's voracious

engine, she imagined she could hear Nick breathing, and hear the strong, steady thud of his heart as it drove blood through his potent, masculine body. She had never felt so connected to another human being in her whole life. Not even, she admitted, that night when she'd been in Nick's bed with her body entwined with his.

It was only when Nick enquired, "Are you sure you're all right, Anna?" that she realized she'd gasped aloud from sensation-overload.

"I'm fine." Her answer was too quick, too sharp. "Don't fuss, Nick. I've got the tiniest bit of a headache, but it's nothing. I'm sure it'll disappear once I get a bit of air."

"I'll stop. We can get out for a while and take a little walk. There's no hurry."

Anna was just about to tell Nick not to worry, when she realized they'd already left the sprawling metropolis behind and were now cruising through an elite, gracious residential area where large, beautifully maintained and very desirable properties bordered the gliding, evening-gilded river. Without further consultation, Nick slowed the mighty car to a halt.

"But Martin will be waiting," Anna protested as Nick slipped out of the car, strode round to the passenger side and flipped up the dramatic door for her. He muttered something succinct and expressively profane in Italian and reached for her hand to assist her from the low-slung seat.

Anna knew she should make a stand, but she couldn't summon the energy. Resisting Nick, even in the most trivial way, was like trying to surf against a riptide. He was simply too big a personality to hold out against.

Looking around, she found that they were on a broad, tree-lined road leading down towards the river. They probably weren't all that far from their destination, the exclusive

Thames-side restaurant, La Girandole, yet suddenly that was the last place she wanted to be.

Walking with Nick on this quiet golden evening was infinitely preferable to facing the awkward confrontation ahead. The cool, rainy conditions of yesterday had been replaced by the brighter flags of early summer. Even the birds were singing, she noticed, and as she turned to Nick, realizing that he showed no intention of letting loose her hand, she accepted that being free of him was last thing she wanted.

"Let's walk a while," he suggested, "Let's pretend we're making the *passeggiata* around the piazza at Fontazone, and I'm showing you off and every male in sight is envious."

With a pang, Anna clearly remembered evenings spent that way, although at the time she'd not been aware of the showing-her-off element. Back then, they'd been easy and comfortable with each other—until she'd screwed up their relationship with her foolish infatuation and her even more idiotic actions. She'd never felt prouder than during those evening perambulations around that small, pretty square, with its busy cafes and shops and cozy family restaurants. Life had been sweet, strolling on the arm of one of the most handsome men in Italy, and to her, the most handsome in the entire world.

"What about the car?" she asked, almost overwhelmed by the poignant recollections. But Nick simply clicked the alarm button on his key fob.

"If anyone so much as breathes on it, we'll hear the alarm from about a mile away." He gave a confident nod. "Not to mention the fact that the glass is bullet-proof and the security system probably the most sophisticated in the world."

"Impressive," she murmured, not so much bothered about the car and its advanced technology, as the painful twist of nostalgia when he tucked her arm in his and smiled at her, just as he had done back in Fontazone.

They walked for a while in silence, each seemingly lost in thought. Anna wondered if Nick had Maria Rossi on his mind. The Italian actress kept stealing into her own thoughts too, along with images of how close, how intimately close Maria and Nick had looked on the television. How much simpler everything would be if Carlo had taken a shine to Maria instead? That way Nick and his gorgeous actress could be engaged for real now, while she could go her own way and set about finding a nice, steady relationship with someone safe and unremarkable.

"No!"

The thought stopped her in her tracks, both literally and figuratively. Her footsteps faltered and she felt Nick pause beside her, even though she didn't dare look at him.

*I don't want a nice, steady relationship with someone unremarkable.*

The words rang in her head so loudly she could almost hear them. She didn't want that kind of relationship. She'd never really wanted it. What she did want was wild, turbulent passion, complete with its frantic lows and its transcendent, ecstatic heights. She wanted to dare to dream that such a relationship could last.

There was only one man she'd ever take that gamble with. And that was the one who was at her side right now, with his warm hand closed around hers in a silent question. A question he was going to ask if she didn't look at him soon.

"What's wrong, Anna?"

*Too late.*

"Is it your headache? Do you want to go home?"

Anna tried to think fast, even though the headache in question was niggling at her. What could she say that wouldn't sound like a lie or evasion? She forced a bright smile.

"Nothing's wrong." She kept her voice level, and as unwavering as the fixed, tense smile that was already making her face ache. "Just something I should have done at work today. No big deal, really. I can see to it tomorrow."

Nick tilted his head, his fine blue eyes narrowing. "Are you sure? We can go back to your office right now, if you want?"

He didn't believe her—that much was obvious. Throughout all the time she'd known him, he'd always exhibited a sixth sense about being deceived, and Anna had no doubt that uncanny power was working now. And yet still, for his own reasons, he was playing along with her.

"No. Thanks. It's okay, really." She tried to sound unconcerned, "Let's just walk on for a few minutes, shall we? Then we'd better be getting to the restaurant. We don't want to keep Martin waiting."

At the sound of Martin's name, Nick's mouth and jaw tightened.

*What? This meeting is your idea, and now you're the one exhibiting reluctance?*

Nevertheless, Nick inclined his gilded head in agreement. Re-tucking her hand under his arm, he urged her forward along the road without speaking.

It should have been an idyllic stroll, but it was tension, tension, tension. Every nerve in Anna's body felt as if it was strung out to breaking point. Every emotion surging through her mind seemed to be in conflict with a dozen others. Every moment that passed, she seemed to be sinking further into a pit of emotional deception and the avoidances of issues.

And then she glanced to her right and saw something lovely, something distracting. It didn't take her attention completely from the tall, powerful figure at her side, but it

108

certainly claimed a little bit of it.

It was a house. A long, sprawling, rather odd-looking house, built from pink-tinted brick that seemed to glow rosy in the sinking sun. Poignant nostalgia gripped her again even though she'd never set eyes on the place before—because she realized in an instant it reminded her of Villa Rosa.

Villa Rosa, Nick's favorite of all his several homes across the world—the modest, unpretentious farmhouse near Fontazone in Liguria. It too had that rambling, relaxed, almost shambolic feel about it, despite the fact that it was in fact furnished with every modern convenience. And the ruddy tint of its weathered brick walls was uncannily similar to that of this Thames-side residence.

Unable to stop herself, she glanced at Nick and saw that he too was staring fixedly at the large, but homely pink house with an expression of surprised recognition on his face.

Even as she watched him, his attention flitted from point to point. The red-tiled roof, the climbing wisteria, the light glinting off the not quite symmetrical windows, and especially on the one on the second floor, at the far end of the building, which just might have been the window to his old room at Villa Rosa.

The room where they'd slept together for the first, and probably the last ever time.

"*Ché bella casa.*"

The sound of his own voice almost surprised him. The unconventional pink house had produced the strangest effect, its odd familiarity and resemblance to Villa Rosa flooding him with instant homesickness.

And more than that. He experienced an odd sensation in the region of his heart, a kind of nostalgia, a physical yearning for a past that had never happened.

Just like Villa Rosa, this quintessentially English "villa" was obviously a family home. The gardens were lush already, and as shambling in their own way as the house itself. He saw a swing, a sandpit, even a set of goalposts, and the faint sparkle of water, possibly a pool. Images leapt instantly into his mind, pictures of a life he'd never even considered before. A life he'd long ago forsworn in the bitter aftermath of his parents' volcanic marriage.

He imagined pushing a small boy on that swing. He pictured a bold, sturdy little child, full of heart and spirit, shrieking with glee and demanding that *Papà* push him higher and higher, the evening sunlight glinting on his golden hair.

Nearby, a chubby girl child played contentedly in the sandpit, flinging the grains high into the air with a spade and laughing with the same inhibited joy as her brother. The tiny girl's hair was darker than her brother's, tawny like his own, and as she seemed to fix on him, cooing with pleasure, he observed, in shock and awe, that her twinkling eyes were the most intense shade of green.

And even as the impact of this revelation rocked him in his handmade shoes, he saw beyond the cherubic child, and his eyes locked with the equally green gaze of the little girl's mother. She was sitting on a spread blanket, relaxed and serene as she raised a slender, elegant hand and flicked her short blonde hair out her eyes and smiled back towards him...

No! *Per dio*, no!

This was not possible. Would never be. He could never allow himself the luxury. For him, such marital bliss would never be a reality, because of his nature, and the legacy of domestic strife that bore down upon him.

More shaken than he wanted to admit, he glanced sideways, at Anna, and his sense of horror was compounded.

She too was staring dreamily at the house, something soft and yearning in her eyes telling him more surely than words that she was seeing the same vision, or her version of it. She even seemed about to poke her face through the tall, wrought iron gate for a better look.

About to speak, Nick suddenly experienced an even more disturbing revelation.

What if he wasn't in this beguiling domestic scene with her? What if was Martin Johnson instead?

Clamping his jaw, Nick bit back a spontaneous cry of outrage and felt his fists curl. Employing a supreme effort of will, he imperceptibly relaxed his almost painfully tense muscles.

What good did this fury he felt do him? He couldn't offer Anna the beautiful, golden future he sensed they were both seeing. So why should she not anticipate it with another man? She was entitled to.

But not with Johnson. Never with that man. He simply wasn't good enough for her.

"It's for sale," he heard Anna murmur, as if from a great distance, and following her eye-line, he saw the discreet estate agent's board planted in a corner of the garden.

"So it is," he drawled, instantly hating the hard, sardonic note in his own voice. "Were you thinking that Johnson might buy it for you as your future family home? A nest in which to raise a clutch of little solicitors, perhaps?"

Anna leapt away from him as if he'd struck her.

"Don't be ludicrous, Nick," she cried, her eyes flashing emerald sparks at him, the perfect curves of her face as set and hard as his were. "I was merely making an observation. And anyway, a house like this, in a location like this, is probably worth millions. Neither Martin, nor I could ever afford it."

111

The sound of the other man's name on her lips was like a poker in the gut to Nick. He felt the demon of his anger raging against its bonds inside him. The irrational possessiveness fulminated and surged.

"And sadly, I don't think your father could bankroll you either, could he?"

Why, oh why was he saying these things?

"Perhaps I should buy the house for the two of you?" he added, "As a gift...a recompense...for services rendered?"

"That's it! I've had enough!"

Turning on her heel, Anna strode away from him, back the way they'd come, her own fury making a rigid line of her straight, elegant spine. "Take me home immediately. I'll phone Martin and I'll explain everything to him privately," she flung over her shoulder, "I'm not subjecting him to you when you persist in behaving like a pig."

Raw shame washed through Nick. She was right. He was behaving like a boor and an irrational idiot. And yet still the thought of her with Johnson lay a red mist across his vision.

"What, would you make him look a fool? Stood up at an expensive restaurant?"

He aimed the words at her beautiful back. "Surely, if you hold him in such high regard, you'll at least have the decency to turn up now and save his feelings?"

Anna spun round again, her eyes still mutinous and her rosy mouth a thin, angry line. In a brief, telling gesture, she rubbed a fingertip against her temple, then drew a deep breath as if fighting a momentary pain.

*Dannazione!* Had he made her ill now?

"I'm sorry. I shouldn't have said that. Of course I'll take you home," he said quietly. He was making a disaster of this evening, and they'd not even reached their destination. He'd take Anna home, and he'd keep his mouth shut until he had her safely at her door.

Moving towards her, he reached to take her arm, but still she bristled away from him. The manifest revulsion in the way she looked at him was like a dagger through his heart.

"No," she shot at him, beautiful green eyes acquiring a steely, determined cast, "We'll go to the restaurant. We'll meet Martin. And we'll get this dismal business over with."

With one last, baleful glance at him, she began walking back to the Vampiro again. Not turning, she continued to speak, "But just remember, Nick. I'm doing this for Carlo, and Carlo alone. None of it's for you."

*I believe you*, thought Nick as his long stride caught him up to her. *I believe you.*

But why do I keep wishing things were different? Why do I keep wishing that my dream of the pink house was real?

# Chapter Six

The evening had begun well. Astonishingly well. But with hindsight, Anna knew it could never have lasted.

Lying in the luxurious, darkened room, she pressed the cool pack against the stabbing ache in her head and tried to stop herself wondering what was happening now.

Had Martin accepted her decision and left with good grace? Or had he decided to take issue with Nick out in the car park or wherever?

A disturbing image of an agitated hyena yipping around a lordly and disdainful King of the Jungle made her smile, despite its inherent awfulness. Alas, the smile only made her head hurt more, and the following frown only piled on the agony throbbing behind her temple.

Conversation had flowed amenably at first, mainly thanks to the Vampiro. Their arrival in the fabulous car had caused a stir throughout the entire hotel, it seemed, and despite the fact he drove a fairly average saloon himself, Martin had seemed entranced by the beautiful supercar. He'd come out into the car park to admire it, and he and Nick had seemed to get on quite amenably as they discussed the car's advanced features. While Anna waited with bated breath, wondering if Nick would suddenly turn the talk a different way.

It was only when they'd returned to the restaurant,

however, and been shown to their table, that the atmosphere had begun to prickle and the conversation had stalled. Nick's frown had been full of concern when she'd politely refused wine in favor of water, but a moment later he'd launched directly into his proposal.

And poor Martin's jaw had literally dropped.

"I'm sorry, Martin," murmured Anna, shifting painfully in an attempt to find a cooler area of the crisp cotton pillowcase, "You didn't stand a chance. You never did."

He'd tried hard enough—she had to give him that. Her now former boyfriend had done his utmost to put on a good showing against his wealthier more cosmopolitan rival. Martin had turned up in a smart, if undistinguished suit, in a clear attempt not to be outdone in the style stakes, but he'd been instantly eclipsed by Nick's effortless, bred-in-the-bone Italian elegance.

And in the ensuing war of words that followed Nick's unadorned announcement of his intentions, Martin's usual solicitor's fluency and his cogent way of putting things had seemed to disintegrate in the face of Nick's low, assured tones. And his supreme, patent certainty that he was going to get exactly what he wanted. As he always did.

"But this is crazy!" Martin's voice had shot up in pitch and he'd nervously crumpled the napkin he'd been in the act of unfolding, "Surely you're not seriously considering this, are you, Anna? What on earth will my mother say?"

*I don't care what your mother says! It's what you think...and feel.*

Controlling her urge to protest, Anna tried to explain her debt of gratitude to Carlo for his many years of kindness. Not an easy task in the face of Martin's confused and astonished interruptions and Nick's silent, intense watchfulness.

*Oh yes, it's all right for you! You calmly fling a lighted match*

115

*into a powder keg, then sit back to enjoy the explosion.*

Eventually, after several minutes of to-ing and fro-ing between Anna and Martin, Nick finally inserted a comment.

"But it's merely going to be a performance. For my father's benefit."

His tone was soft and silky. "Call it an engagement of convenience, if you will. Nothing more than an arrangement between two old friends. There's no question of it being anything more intimate."

*Oh that's great! Just great!* raged Anna silently, wincing from a pulse of pain behind her left eye, the unmistakable harbinger of a full-on migraine. *If you hadn't mentioned it, it might never have entered Martin's head. But now it's the only thing he'll be able to think of.*

Which it clearly now was.

"I should jolly well think not!"

Martin was on his feet, his usual mild-mannered demeanor a thing of the past, and his face red with anger and suspicion.

Anna glanced from him towards Nick, and for a split second she caught a hint of devilish triumph in those shimmering blue eyes.

She wanted to slap him. Hard.

And the glint was still there as he quietly excused himself, offering them a few moments of privacy for their discussions while he had a word with the hotel owner, an old friend of his.

He'd done it on purpose; Anna had no doubt of that. He wanted to split her and Martin up for real, and this was the sure-fire way to do it.

And he'd succeeded.

Anna sighed into the pillow, gripped by the migraine that had developed with alarming rapidity, accelerated by the increasingly acrimonious conversation over their uneaten, untouched food. Despite her best efforts to clarify a situation that couldn't be less clear if she'd actively *tried* to complicate it, Martin had grown more and more hostile, and in all honesty Anna couldn't blame him.

How would she have reacted in his place? Just as angrily, no doubt.

When he'd finally laid down his ultimatum, it had come as a relief. The manifestation of something she'd already been contemplating, nay, planning to do long before she'd opened the door just yesterday evening and let Niccolo Lisitano step back into her life...and her heart.

"If you must go through with this ridiculous charade, I really don't think we ought to go on seeing each other, Anna," Martin had intoned.

He'd sounded aggrieved and deflated, yet it seemed he'd given in after only the first skirmish. Perversely, Anna knew if he'd stuck to his guns and fought for her, something might have been salvaged between them. "I can't expose Mother to the possible embarrassment. And I have my own reputation to consider."

A thought crystallized in her mind with such piercing clarity that it almost seemed like a gouging new manifestation of her headache. She groaned, low and soft, as she examined it.

If the positions had been reversed, Nick *would* have fought for her and crushed all opposition. The only reason she'd ever started seeing Martin—and men like him—was because in every way that mattered he was the antithesis of Nick.

For wildly differing reasons, she knew that neither arrogant, glamorous Nick nor quiet, self-effacing Martin were the perfect man for any woman. But in her heart, she knew which one she'd follow to the ends of the earth and beyond.

As she turned restlessly against the pillow, even that very slight movement ratcheted up the pain level appallingly. It became a hot haze in her brain, consuming her last ounce of energy and her every scrap of consciousness.

Yet as she surrendered to it, she accepted she'd made the right decision.

Nick strode along the corridor almost at a run, anxious to get back to the suite he'd secured for Anna as soon as he'd realized what was the matter with her.

His friend Gian-Baptiste had been glad to oblige, even though La Girandole was virtually fully booked for the night. They were lucky that just one particular suite was available.

Pausing with his hand on the doorknob, Nick ran his hand through his hair, wondering if he should have thrown as much money as was needed at the problem and secured himself separate accommodation.

On balance, he decided it was better not to. Anna might object violently to sharing a suite with him once she recovered from her migraine, but for the moment, she was ill and he couldn't leave her to suffer alone for a second longer than was necessary. The image of her chalk-white face and the lines of pain etched across her beautiful features as he'd scooped her up and carried her bodily from the restaurant were seared into his memory.

He let himself into the room with the absolute minimum of noise, and then padded through the elegant sitting room, and into the darkened bedroom beyond. The irony of where he was brought a twisted smile to his lips. Though the circumstances were far from romantic, he and his new "fiancée" were now lodged in La Girondole's honeymoon suite.

All he could see of Anna was a small mound beneath

luxuriously embroidered ivory counterpane of the huge, canopied four-poster bed. She had the bedclothes over her head, presumably to keep out every scrap of agonizing light, and as soundlessly as he could, Nick pushed the door behind him closed in order to exclude the illumination of the sitting room.

Coming closer, he felt frustrated in a way that was totally alien to him. One of his greatest strengths was his ability to solve problems, but in this situation what could he really do to help Anna?

How could he take away the pain? If he so much as sat on the edge of the bed and tried to speak to her, the movement and the sound would only exacerbate her suffering. He'd never felt powerless before in his life, and he didn't like the feeling. He suddenly wished with all his heart that he could simply assume the accursed migraine in her place.

A tiny sound, somewhere between a sigh and moan, issued from beneath the bedclothes, and at the same time there was movement beneath them. Plucking at the knees of his perfectly tailored trousers, Nick sank down to a kneeling position beside the bed and held his breath, wondering if a few reassuring words would help...or be rejected.

Slowly, Anna's ashen face emerged from beneath the ivory silk, looking like an even paler oval in the faint veil of moonlight seeping in through the curtains. Her green eyes were dark and clouded, her shining hair ruffled and her soft mouth pinched with pain. With obvious effort, she frowned for a second, and then the ghost of a smile formed on her lips.

Her voice, when she managed to speak, was thin and reedy, but Nick still detected a distinct mocking edge that irrationally cheered him.

"What on earth are you doing down there? Kneeling in

prayer for my recovery?"

Nick returned her effort at a smile, his fingertips on fire with the urge to stroke her face and hair soothingly, yet all the while knowing that contact might not be welcome.

"Well, if you think it'll help, yes, I'll try it." He kept his voice muted. "But actually I was just trying to see how you are, there in your burrow. Any improvement?"

"No. Not really...but thank you." The words were an obvious struggle.

"Perhaps this will help."

Still kneeling, Nick reached into the jacket of his suit and took out a small white paper bag containing a packet of tablets. Glancing swiftly at the dosage instructions, he popped one out of the foil, and held it towards Anna. When she blinked and looked suspicious, he held up the packet in his other hand.

"How did you get those? They're prescription only," she queried, one slender hand emerging from hiding to take the pill from him. As she slipped it into her mouth, Nick poured water from the carafe on the bedside table, and once she'd struggled to sit, emerging more fully from the covers, he held the half-full glass to her lips as she drank.

"Would you believe that I walked into the crowded restaurant and asked if there was a doctor in the house?"

Relinquishing the glass to him, Anna laughed, then held her head and scrunched up her eyes, clearly regretting her mirth. "I'd believe anything of you," she observed, her voice thin but still amused.

When Nick helped her to lie down again, she didn't hide her head, but simply kept her eyes tightly closed. "Alas, there was no doctor, but a very helpful fellow migraine sufferer suggested I find out what medication you take and obtain some for you."

"And how did you do that?"

"I rang Lydia. She wanted to come down here herself and look after you, but I assured her that you were quite safe in my hands—" Anna made a faint harrumph sound, but Nick ignored her, "—and asked for the name of your medicine. After that, it was a simple matter of ringing a physician friend of mine, who wrote a prescription and arranged for an express motorcycle courier to take the scrip to an all-night chemist and then bring the medicine here."

"Life's very easy when you've got mountains of money and convenient friends, like doctors and hotel owners and suchlike." Anna's voice sounded stronger now, and though he doubted the tablet could have acted so quickly, Nick's heart lifted to hear so much fight returning to her.

"In this case, fortunately for you, yes. Life *is* easier with wealth and connections," he admitted, voice still low, but crisper.

There was a silence, then, "Thank you." The words were soft, but not grudging, totally genuine. Having always enjoyed the rudest good health himself, Nick wondered for a moment what it would be like to be laid so low. "Thank you for looking after me. I don't know what I would have done without you."

*Probably not got the headache in the first place,* thought Nick wryly. But before he could say so, she went on more strongly. "But I *don't* thank you for being so blunt and lacking in tact with Martin. You could have worked up to things a bit more subtly, Nick."

True, but despite the situation, he felt compelled to justify himself. His motives had been sound. Or, it could be just a case of it seemed like a good idea at the time...

"I just wanted to get everything out in the open and dealt with as quickly as possible. So we could all enjoy a pleasant dinner." He paused, fingers still tingling with the urge to reach out and touch her, soothe her pain. "I saw no reason to prolong the agony."

Another harrumph from the depths of the covers pointed out the irony of that remark.

"I suppose he's gone now, hasn't he?" she asked.

"Yes, he's long gone. He made his choice with a surprising alacrity. I was quite impressed with his decision making. And with yours," he finished softly.

"I didn't have a choice, if you remember. You forced the issue."

"You have always been a free agent, Anna," Nick said, aware that out of necessity he *had* maneuvered her. "And yet you chose me over him."

"I didn't choose you." Anna's words sounded tired rather than belligerent. Their conversation was clearly wearing her out. "I chose what was right for Carlo."

"And I thank you for that," Nick answered without hesitation, touched again, thinking of his father in another sick bed in another country, and what Anna's choice—however temporary it was—would mean to him.

"And for Dad too. Don't try and tell me that it's *only* the idea that we're engaged that's making him look as if he's had a huge weight lifted off his shoulders."

Nick admired her pragmatism. It reminded him of his own decision making. Yet he still felt an odd, piqued sensation that made him frown.

Was there nothing personal in this deal for her? Why did she so consistently fight the fact that she still wanted him? She'd been with him all the way last night in the kitchen, so why not own up to her urges? And—just as he hoped to do—

make the most of their enforced togetherness with mutual pleasure. Even if it was only a temporary arrangement?

"Of course," he said more coolly, "although I must point out that an injection of cash for Felgate's was never contingent upon our becoming engaged. It was already a gladly done deal."

"Of course," she echoed. Despite her obvious pain, the cynicism in her thready voice was evident.

"You don't sound as if you believe me?"

"You're a ruthless man, Nick." Her brow puckered, and the tiny action made her wince, "I know you'll do anything to get what you want. You did tonight." She paused, her eyelids fluttering, but not opening. "And I'm just wondering what an injection of cash for my father *might* be contingent upon. I know that it isn't just this mock engagement you're after."

It was Nick's turn to frown, instantly comprehending her meaning. His anger flared. With difficulty, he suppressed an instant outburst, aware the sudden flash of ire was as much directed inward as it was at Anna.

"Don't worry," he said after a moment, forcing the words out between rigid lips, "I don't require you to sleep with me in order for me to help your father. I offer financial aid as Clive's friend, because I respect and care for him."

He drew a quick breath, suddenly aware that he'd been holding that in tightly too. "And I want you to sleep with me because I desire you and you desire me. It's as simple and uncomplicated as that."

Anna plucked at the coverlet, but Nick gently prevented her from pulling it over her head again. She wasn't going to hide from her false accusations, migraine or no migraine.

"You continually cast me in the role of sex-crazed monster, but I'll prove to you that I'm not one." He glanced quickly at the width of the large, canopied bed, assessing its acreage. "I'll

sleep beside you in this bed and I won't even touch you. Will
that prove to you that my intentions are all above board? That
I'm not trying to coerce you into sex?"

*Above board?* Yes. He sincerely meant it. But an intense
bolt of desire, blended with self-loathing, made him catch his lip
between his teeth and wrestle for control. Even as he'd swept
her up and carried her from the restaurant—distraught and in
pain—his wayward body had reacted, tightening and hardening.

Anna turned her face towards the pillow and burrowed into
it, still frowning. Was it from pain? Disbelief? Acceptance? Or
what? When she spoke, her voice was slurred, and Nick realized
the rapid-acting medication was kicking in.

"There's no need for that. I believe you," she mumbled into
the pillow, "Now just leave me alone and go to your own room.
I'll...I'll be all right. I just need sleep." This time when she
fumbled for the edge of the cover, he didn't try to stop her.

"There is no *my* room," he told the hump beneath the
embroidered ivory silk. "This was the last remaining suite,
Anna. We have no choice but to share it."

Even though she was entirely hidden, he sensed immediate
tension in her concealed form. But only for a moment or two.
The anti-migraine drug was too strong, and it had her in its
hold.

As her body relaxed again, he heard a soft and muffled,
"Whatever."

"Whatever," affirmed Nick, knowing she was already asleep
and beyond both pain and their conflict.

But for him there would be no such escape. And the night
ahead would be long with uncomfortable wakefulness.

*I'll sleep beside you in this bed.*

The words popped into Anna's mind the instant she came awake, and they were so astonishing that her heart leapt in shock.

Because they were real.

Opening her eyes, she took in the fact that her headache was gone, and she felt clear and calm. The room around her was faintly illuminated by a muted up-lighter on the far wall, which immediately made her feel safer because she'd never been able to sleep in full darkness since she was a child.

But the most important thing, the most amazing thing, the most terrifying and wonderful thing, was that Nick lay asleep beside her in the wide, luxurious bed.

He wasn't touching her. In fact, there seemed to be yards of mattress separating them. But as she lay in silence, taking in his presence, she could hear the faint sound of his even breathing, and a hint of body warmth was apparent even across the gulf between them.

With slow, infinite care, she turned over to face him...and was instantly catapulted into the past by a sense of breath-catching *deja vu*.

That beautiful face, often so fierce and uncompromising, was gentler, almost angelic in repose. Nick was lying on his back, one arm thrown backwards across the pillow, just as it had been when she'd first entered his bedroom four years ago at Villa Rosa. His gilded hair was tousled and his sculpted lips were parted. There was a soft sheen on his golden skin, as if he'd recently shaved and anointed his face with some kind of balm. His thick dark lashes lay like scimitars across his cheekbones.

But there was a significant difference to that first occasion when she'd joined Nick in his bed.

In Italy, he'd been sensuously naked beneath a single,

125

lightweight sheet.

Here in England, he was chastely swaddled in a thick, fluffy bathrobe, which as far as she could tell, covered quite a significant portion of him.

*Hmm...playing it safe, are we?*

Anna sat up cautiously, trying to move as little as possible so as not to disturb the sleeping Nick. Had he bundled himself up in the robe to avoid inadvertently coming into contact with her while he slept? Or was it the other way round? Was it to stop her reaching for him while she was doped and drowsy?

Either way, he might as well have built the Great Wall of China between them. Last night's confrontation in the kitchen had obviously been a momentary lapse of judgment on his part, one that he wasn't planning to repeat. At least not tonight.

On her part, it'd been pure heaven, and only now, in the silent night, with Nick just inches away from her, did she admit it.

Nick stirred slightly, and Anna froze, fearing he might wake. But all that happened was that he adjusted the position of his broad shoulders against the mattress, and then stilled again, the pure, calm expression on his sleeping face still almost beatific.

Maybe she was misjudging him? He was clearly keeping to his side of the bed and was sleeping in the robe so he wouldn't disturb her. There was no doubt after last night that he did want her, but out of consideration for her illness, he was trying to contain himself, while at the same time proving to her that he could do it.

Pushing her hand through her hair, Anna reflected that Nick suppressing his desire for her at the moment was probably a fairly easy job. She wrinkled her nose in disgust. She was a complete mess. Having simply crawled under the covers fully clothed, her top and trousers were tangled and crumpled around her, and she felt grubby and disheveled and less than fresh. She could well imagine the sorts of spikes and tufts her hairstyle had turned into, and whatever remained of her makeup was probably accenting entirely different parts of her face to the ones to which it had originally been applied.

"Yuk," she mouthed silently.

*I look as if I've slept under a bridge for six months,* she thought, *and he's the prince of fastidious perfection.*

Slowly, and watching Nick for signs of waking with every inch she shifted, Anna slid out of bed and padded towards the en-suite bathroom. There was a nail-biting moment when she switched on the light, but thankfully, it wasn't the sort where the air con started up at the same time, so she was able to slide in, close the door and do something about herself without disturbing her sleeping companion.

The mirror revealed exactly the sight she'd feared.

Her hair was sticking up at all angles, and smears of mascara and eye shadow gave her the appearance of the mutant offspring of a clown and a panda. Her lip tint was nowhere to be seen, and her blusher seemed to have gone AWOL too. She could only hope it wasn't smeared all over the exquisite hotel bedding.

And yet, for all her disastrous appearance, she felt better. It was always like this after a migraine. The sheer relief of not being in pain any more seemed to produce a sense of wellbeing and euphoria that was out of all proportion with the prevailing circumstances. She felt light-spirited, confident and positive.

Yes, she was in a weird situation with Nick, and she'd just broken up with a perfectly nice boyfriend. But still she felt optimistic. She'd deal with Nick somehow and fulfill her part of the deal for the sake his father.

But first, she had to do something about herself.

Twenty minutes later, Anna felt more presentable. She'd washed, then tamed her hair, and cleansed off her makeup and moisturized her face with items from the hotel's luxurious selection of complimentary beauty products. Her trousers and top were hanging up, and hopefully shedding their creases, and she'd even managed to rinse out her underclothes and arranged them over the towel rail to dry.

As she put her hand on the door handle though, her post-migraine super self-confidence wobbled slightly. In that sumptuous bed next door was Nick, the man she loved but who didn't love her. She had to climb between the sheets beside him, and then pretend she didn't want him to wake up and make love to her, even if it was something she did want. With all her heart.

Tiptoeing, she crept towards the bed, then tweaked up the covers and slithered inside. Not too easy when she too was swathed in one of the hotel's supremely thick toweling robes. But on sneaking a surreptitious peak at Nick's sleeping face, she saw no sign that she'd disturbed him. His carved, elegant features remained still and tranquil.

*Mission accomplished*, Anna told herself, acknowledging a vague sense of disappointment. Had she wanted him to wake? To see her recovered and restored to at least some semblance of attractiveness, and then find her irresistible?

*Don't be an idiot. That way lies madness.*

But good sense and rationality had never been a key part of the equation where her dealings with Nick were concerned.

Still, she had to get back to sleep and try and ignore the fact he was there. Even though that was difficult, very difficult. Since that one night at Villa Rosa, she'd never ever shared her bed with anyone.

Eyes closed, she turned her back on him, preparing for the long struggle required to quit wakefulness. For a few seconds, all was quiet, all was perfectly still, and then with a suddenness that made Anna's heart lurch beneath her ribs, the bed shifted and a hand settled oh so lightly on her shoulder.

"How do you feel, Anna? Any better now?"

Nick's voice, usually so crisp and incisive, was blurred around the edges from sleep, and his fluid Italian accent sounded more pronounced than usual. Anna trembled as his long fingers flexed lightly on her terry-clad shoulder. Almost reluctantly, she rolled over in bed to face him.

"Yes. A lot better, thanks. The pill worked a treat. It always does."

The light was faint, but Nick's eyes were luminous, even in semi-shadow.

"*Bene.*"

Even just the two syllables told her he was fully awake now, all fragments of the sleepiness of a moment ago completely dispersed. Nick eased himself up on one elbow, and the hand that had touched her shoulder now settled with infinite gentleness on her recently cleansed cheek.

"*Bene,*" he repeated. His blue eyes were almost navy as he looked down on her, but still dazzling.

"Thanks for looking after me," whispered Anna. Her every nerve was screaming, yet oddly, it wasn't an unpleasant sensation. She felt as if she were teetering on a precipice, but the gulf that stretched beneath her wasn't some horrid, dreaded pit. Instead, a warm and delicious paradise beckoned. If only she dared jump.

"I'm sorry I snarled at you," she went on, mesmerized by

the sight of him above her, looming but not threatening. "It wasn't very gracious of me when you'd been so kind."

Long, long eyelashes flicked down and then up.

"But it was most likely my fault you had the headache in the first place. And my handling of the situation this evening could have been subtler. Martin Johnson is a decent enough man." He paused, the slightest of smiles quirking his full lower lip. "Not right for you, of course, but still decent."

"Yes, he is," Anna said quickly, suddenly not wanting to think about any other man but the one in bed with her again after all this time. "But still, I should have shown more gratitude...for you getting me this room and all."

What was going on behind those eyes? Was he about to take that leap too?

"*Molto grazie*, Nick," she murmured, feeling his fingertips burning against her cheek.

"*Prego.*"

Was he moving towards her? Closing in?

Impatience bubbled up. She lifted a hand of her own and curved it against the hard, uncompromising line of his jaw, then around the strong line of his neck to the back of his skull.

There was no need to exert pressure, because he was already lowering his mouth towards hers.

"Are we friends again, then?"

She felt the words against her lips in a feather-light touch and experienced the most piercing shaft of bittersweet sadness.

Friends, yes... They were special friends. As intimate as friends could be. But to Nick, they would never be more, because he didn't want that. Perhaps, would never need it. But Anna did. She wanted and needed love—love from Nick—yet tonight she would accept this, the closest approximation,

130

because she had enough love in her heart for the both of them.

"Yes," she gasped fiercely, giving him his answer, but only managing the single syllable before his kiss overpowered her and stole her ability to speak completely.

# Chapter Seven

Exploring, Anna slid her fingertips down the strong column of Nick's neck and throat, then lower, between the thick, toweling lapels of his robe, to travel over his smooth, broad chest.

His skin was hot, and like satin, oiled satin overlaying sculpted, hard-packed muscle. She hardly dare touch him he was so precious to her, yet her delicate forays evoked a sudden, thrilling response.

A low, murmured growl. Fierce Italian utterances that she didn't understand, despite her fair command of the language, were magical against her lips before his tongue moved into her mouth and spoke even more powerfully and evocatively than words ever could.

It wasn't just her mouth she opened to him, but everything that she was. Impatient, she pulled at his robe and her own, getting the fluffy cloth into a tangle. But Nick's deft hands intervened, performing the task effortlessly, removing the barriers between them. Then he pressed down on her so they were body to body, skin to skin, and groin to groin.

Anna gasped around the possessing invasion of his tongue. Dear Lord, how could she have forgotten? The heat and hardness of him was potent and miraculous against her belly, pressing against the juncture of her thighs. Not yet demanding entrance, but simply letting her know him and feel him and anticipate him—so she would be ready.

Unable to prevent herself, she surged against him, glorying the supreme maleness of his hard body, the potent majesty that moved against her in return.

"Ah, *piccolina*," he breathed, his voice ragged as he freed her mouth and moved his own lower, strafing kisses across her cheek, her jaw and her throat, tasting and nipping.

Anna had always believed that she had every second of that night four years ago seared into her memory. But memory could play tricks, and patterns in the brain were not the real man.

The real Nick, not the phantasm molded by dreams and anguish, was like a force of nature against her, so hungry, kissing her with both assured skill and yet a manic desperation that matched her own. As his lips travelled, moving over her collar bone, then on and down to the slopes of her breasts, his hands voyaged too, rediscovering her back, her flanks, her buttocks, her thighs, sometimes lingering, sometimes skimming with tantalizing lightness.

She groaned softly as he found the crest of her nipple and worried it, his tongue flicking and tormenting, circling, circling, circling before his mouth closed more firmly around the little peak, and he sucked. Anna's soft moan soared to a ragged cry as a jolt of pure pleasure shot from her breast to the aching niche between her legs that cried for Nick's possession. Beyond any kind of control, she writhed, twisting like a mad thing, insane to get more of him, join with him and be one with him.

"Hush, *bella mia*." His mouth was still hot on her breast, the tormenting dart of his tongue belying his soothing words.

But Anna couldn't hush. Murmuring and gasping, she sent her own hands sliding between his burning skin and the toweling that still enveloped them, gliding over his powerful back and the beautifully defined musculature of his buttocks.

He was perfection. Every part of him was a wonder. And as he kissed his way back up to her face, she at last cradled the very essence of what made him man in her fingers.

She loved him. She loved the formidable, blade-like intellect behind that broad sweat-sheened brow. She loved the brave, generous, passionate heart that beat in his magnificent chest. And she loved this, his essential maleness, his fabulous, fabulous body whose unyielding pagan beauty rendered her helpless and longing before him.

"*Si...si...*" His voice was half-growl, half-entreaty, totally compelling, "Yes, Anna *mia*... Yes, caress me," he commanded.

Lost in love, and lust and devotion, she obeyed, shimmering her fingers over him with a skill she barely knew she possessed, working the velvet skin over the steel-hard core, responding instinctively to his gasps and male purrs of satisfaction.

As she caressed him, his long, potent form flexed against hers, and his head tossed just as hers had when he'd sucked her breast in such delicious torment. But at last his larger hand settled over her slender one and gently plucked it from his flesh.

"You have the hands of an angel...and of a witch, *ragazza mia*," he said in a voice that was not quite steady. "Any more of this gorgeous touching and I won't be any good to you." He drew her hand to his lips and kissed it briefly, in tribute.

And then it was his turn to caress, to honor her intimately. Long fingers moved like fire trails over her skin, sliding downwards, downwards towards the moist, yearning delta that craved him.

The contact was like an electric charge against the very centre of her, so light, yet so unerringly accurate and stirring.

Gently, lovingly, he touched and petted her, his fingertip circling there as his tongue had circled her nipple. Anna's hips rose of their own accord, meeting the pressure, inciting it, her entire being reaching for the dazzling moment that glittered in the air before her.

Nearly. Nearly. Nearly. Oh yes!

She cried out sharply as sensation seemed to implode at the very quick of her, its epicenter fluttering beneath Nick's caressing fingers. Agonized with bliss, she clutched him against her, her own fingers helplessly gouging his back as the intense orgasm crested like a wave, flinging her high and bright, then gradually, oh so gradually, floating her down again.

Moments, or perhaps hours, later, Anna found herself collapsed against the mattress, with Nick's softly kissing mouth against her brow, and his hand first stoking her cheek, and then smoothing her hair away from her face.

"You're beautiful, Anna," he whispered, "So sweet...so giving... There's no one like you." She felt the delicate touch of his tongue against her skin as if he were tasting her sweat. "Can you forgive me for the way I behaved last time we were together like this?"

The words were so low, so intense. So real. How could she not forgive him? She would forgive this man anything.

Summoning the strength that seemed to have been blasted from her body by the beauty of her orgasm, she lifted a hand and stroked his lean, carved face in return. Blue eyes like indigo seemed to draw her in, invite her to drown in them, burn again in their fire.

"Of course. Oh yes... Oh Nick, I—" She caught herself. Oh no, she must not say that. It wasn't what he wanted from her.

"I want you, Nick. Please make love to me."

"*Bella mia, bella mia...*" His kisses rained all over her hot face like a benediction. "I want you too... Oh how I want you."

Want. Yes, he wanted her. But that was all. He cared for her too, but in his own way, under his own terms.

Pain enveloped her for a moment. Furious and so powerful and bittersweet that it was as beautiful as it was distressing. Then she banished it and pulled him closer. Yes, he *wanted* her, but she *needed* him. Needed him like the very air she breathed.

"Yes," crowed Nick, kissing her hard on the mouth, before pulling back and swiftly stripping away his own robe and then freeing Anna from hers. In the dim light his body was like a mythical warrior's, both gleaming and intimidating, yet an object of worship. The low light gleamed on his flexing arms and shoulders as he turned from her a moment, investigating the drawer in the bedside cupboard. Complimentary condoms were forthcoming and once he was enrobed, Anna reached for him, beyond impatient now to feel his heated flesh inside her.

Then he moved over her, weight on one elbow while he stroked her face, as if searching by touch for the answer to some new, deep question. She felt his sex resting against her, waiting, waiting.

"Are you sure, Anna?"

His voice was low and thrilling, and his eyes as deep and dark a blue as the edge of space.

*Why ask?*

Yet frantic with need, she still knew why he paused. He was thinking of last time, and how it had shattered their friendship for four long years. Was he afraid that would happen again? Was he giving her the final word, the choice between the two states?

Being friends or being lovers?

*I want both! I want both!* she told him silently, while the single word "yes" formed on her lips.

His answer was immediate, and it came in the form of the magnificent, measured thrust of his body into hers. Anna cried out as he entered her, coiling her arms around him as he filled and stretched the silky, liquid flesh that had yearned for him all through those cold, separated years.

And his eyes were still upon hers. Still asking? Reading her? Comprehending the emotion she felt, which he did not? All of a sudden, Anna couldn't bear to think that anything could divide them, so she clasped him tighter, pressing her mouth against his for a kiss, and caressed him inwardly in the most intimate way she could.

Nick made a low, rough sound against her lips, no words now, just inarticulate expressions of profound response as he began to move, flexing his powerful hips to possess her ever more intensely, in a slow, insistent rhythm. She could sense him exerting almost superhuman control, trying to extend and increase her pleasure.

*I love you,* she thought, her heart wracked again with the painful beauty of it, even as her body, every part of her body it seemed, began the miraculous, barreling climb towards the ultimate peak. She felt a great sensation of gathering and of tightening, each surge of Nick's wonderful body ramping up the inner, glowing pressure. Beyond herself, yet focused completely on being one with him, Anna tossed her head, gasped and whimpered, reaching, reaching for that brilliant prize.

And finally she grasped it, receiving it as a gift into her heart and mind and body, by the grace of the beautiful man making love to her. Hot tears spilled onto her cheeks as just too much exquisite sensation imploded in the very essence of her being.

"I—"

Her mouth against the hard, sweat-sheened muscle of Nick's warm shoulder, she bit down to prevent the telling words of love from revealing her. She tasted blood as with one last, marvelous surge he too grasped the glittering prize and emptied himself, groaning, inside her.

Nick glanced across the cabin of the Lisitano Learjet and found himself rubbing absently at the tiny wound in his shoulder through fabric layers of his suit jacket and his shirt.

It didn't hurt, but somehow every time he looked at Anna, as he was now, he felt again the supreme pleasure that had accompanied the tiny sensual pain.

His sex hardened, recalling the perfection of her naked body. Today, for travelling, she was wearing a pair of snug-fitting jeans and an almost severe white blouse primly buttoned. Yet to Nick, she looked uniquely enticing and arousing. The lush, yet innocent curve of her eyelashes as she peered at the copy of Vogue Italia she was flicking through induced a twist of longing in him that he found difficult to tame. It was erotic, and yet something different, something indefinable.

Fighting for control, Nick watched as Anna frowned at something she was reading, and he felt an immediate urge to press his lips to her puckered brow and banish whatever was vexing her with a soothing kiss.

He'd made a shocking miscalculation. One so disturbing that had the equivalent taken place in his business dealings he would have lost thousands, possibly millions.

The physical reunion that he and Anna had shared had rocked him to his core. He'd never expected it to reach so deep inside him.

Anna was undoubtedly beautiful—as lovely as an angel—and even four years ago, unschooled, she'd been a remarkable lover. But that strange, accidental, almost unlooked-for night at La Girandole had been a revelation. The way she'd responded to him. Her unique intensity. The magical way she'd touched him and enveloped him and almost climbed inside his living soul had shaken everything he'd previously believed about sex and women.

Nick had enjoyed some pretty spectacular nights with some exceptional women in the four years since the teenaged Anna had stolen into his bed at Villa Rosa, but not one of them had unnerved him the way she had.

And she unnerved him now.

He'd thought he could read her easily, but all of a sudden she'd become opaque to him. Oh, she'd been affectionate enough after they'd made love, tender even, but she'd still maintained a subtle almost indefinable distance. There had been no fireworks and recriminations after this coupling. But there had been no clinging either. No staking of claims. No female territory marking. She acted as if they were exactly what they'd said they were.

Friends.

Friends who'd made love. Friends who were working together on a project.

Which was precisely what he wanted, wasn't it? What he'd hoped for. Part of the plan. He'd reasoned with himself that they could enjoy each other for the duration of their fake engagement, and that's just what they were doing. And afterwards they'd part again amicably. He would move on to his next partner, as he always did. And Anna, sensually primed and freed from her unfulfilling relationship with Martin Johnson, would find a man who could meet all her needs and expectations, both physically and emotionally. Maybe even a man she could marry and spend her life with?

That sensation Nick found hard to name surged inside him again, tightening and coiling. To the point of pain. He smoothed his fingers over the fine silk-mix of his jacket again, massaging his non-painful shoulder as if trying to induce a real discomfort that might distract him.

Dangerous thoughts threatened to well up and he mustn't allow them to. That way lay disaster for Anna—and for him.

Awareness prickled through Anna's body.

Placing her fingers across the face of Maria Rossi, who had been gazing up at her with sultry insolence from the Italian fashion spread, she looked up and glanced across at Nick. Exactly as her sixth sense had predicted, he was looking back at her with unnerving intensity.

Mad heat surged through her body, and she felt an imbalance somewhere in her mid-section that had nothing to do with airsickness.

Time after time, in the last couple of hurried days while they'd been preparing for this whistle-stop trip to Italy, she'd caught Nick staring at her with this same odd assessing expression on his face. Asking the same questions with his laser blue eyes, the ones that never seemed to reach his sculpted lips. Even though he'd barely touched her—other than in the most circumspect, social way—since two nights ago.

"What?" she demanded without thinking, meeting his gaze as boldly.

"I was just about to tell you that we'll be landing at Cristofero Colombo in a few minutes. You seem to be deeply absorbed in your magazine."

How could he sound so cool, so detached, after the conflagration that had raged between them in bed? In a lot of ways, it barely seemed to have affected him, while for her...well...everything had changed.

Biting her lip, she looked down at the magazine again. Maybe *there* was the reason that their night together hadn't rocked his world as it had rocked hers.

"Wouldn't you be?" she suggested tartly, holding up the page for him to see.

Nick gave her a bland look, still apparently unmoved, even by the sight of a woman who might, or might not, still be his real girlfriend. Exceptional sex might be something he enjoyed with La Rossi too. The Italian actress was an internationally acclaimed beauty and one of the world's most sensual film stars.

After a long pause, Nick sighed.

"Yes, Maria is a friend of mine, as you well know."

"Oh. Really. And are you *friends* the way that you and I are *friends?*"

*What* is *the matter with me?* Anna fought the urge to crumple the glossy pages.

*I mustn't show him I'm jealous and I mustn't show him how I really feel. It won't get me anywhere and it'll only cause friction between us.* Friction was something Carlo would spot, no matter how ill he was. Not to mention everybody else who was supposed to be taken in by this charade.

Nick seemed unfazed by her accusation.

"There are different of kinds of friendships, Anna," he said evenly, his hand lifting momentarily to his shoulder, as if to remind her of the character of their particular relationship. Anna felt a fresh rush of heat, remembering...

"And no two are the same," Nick went on, calmly reaching for the buckle of his seatbelt. "Now buckle up. We're landing in a minute." His crisp, businesslike tone indicated that for him at least, the discussion was over.

But demons seemed to have taken command of Anna's tongue. "It *was* her, wasn't it? The one who phoned when we were at Deighton Industries?"

A plume of backhanded satisfaction shot through her at the sight of Nick's suddenly quelling glance. She'd rather it hadn't been Maria Rossi—even though she knew unequivocally that it had been—but at least she'd got some kind of reaction from him!

"Maria needed some advice from me, and naturally I needed to see her in person." The moment of irritation, or whatever it had been, was gone as fast as it'd appeared, and once more he wore his beautiful, unrevealing mask. "I would have done exactly the same for you if the tables had been turned. Now please fasten your safety belt. Or do I have to fasten it for you?"

*Come on then!* she wanted to challenge him. *Either that, or just stop treating me like a child. I was grown up enough for you the other night.*

But instead, she just said, "Of course." Then, setting aside the magazine with controlled, tightly buttoned-up care, she reached for the buckle of her belt.

For a VIP like Nick, airport formalities were relatively painless, and in no time at all they were speeding out of the city of Genoa towards the exclusive private clinic where his father was recovering.

The back seat of the luxurious Lisitano limousine was almost as spacious and well-appointed as the Learjet had been, but Anna still felt oppressed and claustrophobic despite the opulence. Nick was working his way through the briefcase full of papers that one of his personal assistants had handed him at Cristofero Columbo Airport, and the fact that his attention was now elsewhere should have been a respite.

But it wasn't. His presence and proximity seemed to bear down on Anna, almost physically pressing on her skin and sensitizing it, and she could only thank her lucky stars that Nick had deemed it impractical for the two of them to return to Italy in the Vampiro.

"I'm sure you'd enjoy the ride," he'd told her, his blue eyes thoughtful, almost wary. "But alas, my vampire car has next to no boot, and I doubt what little space there is could accommodate even a fraction of the luggage required by the average woman, even for a trip of a few days."

On the point of rebuking him for male chauvinist preconceptions, Anna had held her tongue and dismissed the remark with a nervous laugh. Boot space wasn't the issue at all. Distance between them was. And she sensed Nick was just as leery as she was of the enforced intimacy of the Vampiro's compact interior.

The vast acreage in the Lisitano Lusso limousine was bad enough.

Even though she'd always enjoyed the Ligurian countryside—a tapestry of vineyards and lemon and olive groves once they'd left the Genoese sprawl—there seemed to be nowhere to look but the interior of the quietly gliding car. Nick's long legs stretched out in front of him, far too close to hers.

Sealed in by steel and tinted glass, Anna felt as if she were in a capsule of compressed tension, with Nick at its heart. His subtle cologne was intensified by the confined space, and it was seeping into her brain and intoxicating her, warping her back to the night at La Girandole, and the feel of that hard, beautiful body clasped against her. He might be clad in another of his dark, exquisitely tailored suits, but she was just as aware of him as she would have been if he'd been stark naked and lying on top of her.

"Speak then, if you're going to."

Nick's sudden, faintly impatient words made Anna physically leap in her seat. Clearly his attention had not been entirely on the papers and files he'd been steadfastly working through. His Mont Blanc hovered over a document as he looked up and fixed her with blue, questioning stare.

"What do you mean?"

Nick's eyes narrowed, and in what looked like long-suffering gesture, he capped his elegant pen and laid it down in his briefcase, which he set aside in the limousine's capacious foot well.

"Anna, you've been staring at me non-stop for the last fifteen minutes at least. I'm guessing that means you want to speak to me?"

He crossed one long, lean leg over the other and stretched his arms out across the back of the seat, the action blatant and challenging. Daring her to look more, look closer, to ogle him in all his male pulchritude.

"I wasn't staring," she fibbed, "And even if I was, how could you tell, you've had your nose stuck in your work since we touched down." Wild heat surged through her veins, triggered by the lie and by the deceptive indolence of his pose.

"A man can always tell when a woman is checking him out. Especially one he's sleeping with."

"*Slept* with," she corrected him, "There's only been the once...and four years ago...and that other thing. In the kitchen."

"Surely that's not going to be all, is it?" He cocked his head to one side, his brilliant eyes narrowing. "You still want me. I still want you. We're still *friends*." His emphasis on the word was silken, almost insulting, and for a moment he looked impossibly predatory. Then his expression softened and became kinder.

"You know how much I care for you, Anna." He sat up and leant towards her. "And we're good together. Surely we can take some pleasure in each other for a while?"

One long hand reached out, curved against her cheek, perfectly matching its contour. The pad of his thumb brushed her lips, light as the kiss of a butterfly, yet supreme in its dominance of her response. Against every command from her higher brain, Anna found herself leaning into the pressure, wanting to kiss not only his thumb and his hand, but every last bit of him. Within the space of only seconds, he'd rendered her entire body a slave to her senses.

The back of the car was a cocoon. They were cut off from the driver and the world by one-way tinted glass. A vision of falling into his arms and his kisses and his total possession here on this soft, fragrant leather upholstery bloomed fully formed in Anna's mind. Her body primed itself for him, and she gasped as her nipples suddenly felt tight and aching beneath her starchy blouse, and lower down she grew shockingly moist and honeyed. The pressure of Nick's thumb delicately increased and her lips parted, tasting his skin.

Desire, the same raw emotion she'd experienced two nights ago, catapulted through her, unrestrained and uninhibited, all connection to good sense and better judgment now severed.

Anna could only feel and want and—yes—love. She sucked on Nick's thumb and slumped like an unstrung puppet against the back of the seat, aware of him following her momentum and making a small sound of male satisfaction as he reached for her with his free hand. Edging his body ever closer to hers, he permitted the evocative caress a moment longer and then gently removed his hand and pressed his parted lips over Anna's.

Oh, how she'd longed for this kiss.

For the two whole days since La Girandole they'd shadow-danced around each other, and every fiber of Anna's being had yearned for the taste and touch of Nick. Whimpering, she allowed him to commandeer her mouth, her tongue—darting and subduing her with his own tongue and with the intense force of the kiss. He too had been yearning, she knew it. He too had been waiting for the fire, kindled originally here in Italy, to break its bounds.

Feeling as if they were sliding into their rightful place, her arms snaked around him, hands inveigling their way beneath his jacket, slipping between its pure silk lining and the fine cotton lawn of his dazzling white shirt. She gasped under the onslaught of his mouth, almost shocked by the pagan heat of his skin through the insubstantial fabric. And as he drew her yet closer, she felt that same heat burning through the layers of her own clothing and his shirt, scorching the aching, puckered tips of her breasts as they pressed against the hard, unyielding wall of his chest.

He was like a rare, vintage wine to her, delicious and intoxicating, full of dangerous power that warped her ability to reason. When she felt him plucking at the buttons of her blouse her hands flew to help him, tugging and pulling at them until the garment was open. Wrenching the panels of fabric apart, she offered her near-naked breasts to him. Her delicate bra was like vapor, and no barrier to speak of between her and his nimble, narrow-tipped fingers.

Anna groaned as he cupped one breast and flicked his

thumb insistently over the crest, strumming it, inciting it to a greater and more aching sensitivity. Between her legs she felt a jolt of heat and a kind of calling flutter, her intimate flesh crying out to him. Wanting his touch.

Driven by desire, Anna scissored her thighs, moving to ease the ache at her feminine core, moving to incite and entice, to draw Nick's hand. She heard his groan, an echo of her own voice, and felt the vibration of it in her mouth. The fingertips that had fondled her breasts slid down, down, down, to settle and then grip possessively at the delta of her sex through the sturdy, hindering denim of her jeans.

The rough, almost primal contact made her jack-knife, and in a fraction of a second, the very quick of her convulsed in a series of hard, intense contractions. A virtually instant orgasm, her need had been so great.

Sobbing against his lips, she clawed at his back through his shirt, one hand sliding down to clasp at his tight male buttock, instinctively pulling closer and trying to feel his erection against her.

Still pulsing, she reached her goal, but it was wrenched away from her as Nick dragged himself back along the seat, rudely separating their bodies and their mouths.

"*Dannazione!*" he muttered, lifting the hands that had caressed her to run them through his gilded hair, once, twice, ruffling it wildly. His eyes were black as the night sky, his high, elegant cheekbones flagged with heat.

Through eyes hazed with confusion, pain and after-pleasure, Anna looked at him and thought him more beautiful and more male than she'd ever seen him.

"What the hell is wrong with me?" he demanded, though to her ears, the accusation was aimed at her. "I haven't groped a woman in the back seat of a car like a hormone-crazed teenager

147

since I *was* a hormone-crazed teenager."

Frozen herself, Anna watched as Nick closed his eyes for a moment, long lashes sweeping down like fans as he seemed to center himself. Then, the fugue of sexual fervor appeared to drain out of him, leaving his face cool and almost distant as he straightened up, smoothed some order back into his mussed up hair, and then adjusted the set of his jacket.

When he looked back at her his blue eyes were as clear and blank as ice.

"You'd better tidy yourself up." His voice was clipped and as expressionless as his face.

Yet still she couldn't move. How could he suddenly be so cold? Surely he'd been as stirred as she'd been. Dear Lord, she'd felt it. His erection had been hard as a bar of iron against her.

But even that seemed to have subsided, she realized, unable to prevent herself glancing down at his groin, her fingers, suddenly all thumbs, plucking ineffectually at her shirt buttons.

Something indefinable flared in his blue gaze as he tracked her eye line, then his spectacular mouth thinned and he edged impatiently towards her.

"Anna, we're nearly at the clinic. Please cover yourself." In an impatient gesture, he dashed her fumbling fingers aside and began to re-button her disheveled white shirt.

Snapping to life at last, she in turn knocked his hands away and fastened herself up with a haste and efficiency fuelled by anger.

"I can manage, thank you very much, Nick," she said crisply, restoring order as best she could.

If only it was as easy to restore order to her senses and her heart. Every time she was around him, in close proximity, she seemed to lose all control on her judgment and sense of self. All she could do was to throw her body at his. Like some crazy person who could only think with parts of herself that were fatally prone to bad decisions.

"And as for this business of being 'friends', and 'taking pleasure in each other', I'm not so sure that it's such a good idea if you think it gives you carte blanche to maul me and manhandle me whenever the fancy takes you."

She secured the last button and twitched her shirt collar a little further up her throat. "I think we should keep this...this arrangement strictly businesslike from now on." She paused, her chin up defiantly. "As it was supposed to be in the first place."

Nick's eyes slid insolently over her, and Anna's ire flared. What was the matter with him? Was he thinking he could start all over again?

"What happened a moment ago was entirely mutual," he observed, as blandly as if he'd been observing the passing scenery. "You were the one who turned to flame in my arms, Anna." His voice deepened to dark velvet. "You were the one who had an orgasm and rubbed herself against me like a cat on heat."

Her hand whipped back ready to strike, but Nick anticipated her and caught her wrist before she had chance to complete the motion.

"Oh no you don't," he said, teeth gritted, even though his body language remained composed. "It wouldn't do to meet my father and his doctors with my cheek red from a slap, would it?"

Gently but unequivocally, he brought her arm down and then released it.

At that moment, Anna could cheerfully have gone fifteen

149

rounds with him and felt so angry, confused and fired up that she might have won. But instead she summoned reserves of sense and self-possession that had been sadly unavailable a few minutes ago.

"Perhaps not," she said coolly, then reached for her bag and drew out a compact and comb. With focused care, and studiously ignoring Nick, she tidied her own untidy hair and checked her face. Thank goodness she'd been wearing a minimum makeup and only needed to replace the slick of clear gloss that had disappeared somewhere during their turbulent kisses.

When she returned her attention to her antagonist, he gave her another long, assessing look, then a small nod as if to say "you'll do".

The urge to strike him funneled up inside her again, but again, she quelled it. She was a grown woman, not a headstrong kid prone to scrapping and fisticuffs.

She took a deep breath, and as she held Nick's gaze as bravely as she could, he shrugged, and then reached down into his abandoned briefcase and pulled out a small, cube-shaped leather-covered box.

Anna knew what it was and felt all the last remnants of fight drain out of her.

"You'd better put this on," said Nick, his voice suddenly weary and resigned sounding as he flipped open the little box to reveal a ring.

# Chapter Eight

For perhaps the hundredth time in a day, Anna glanced down at the ring.

It was a thing of beauty—a flawless cabochon ruby cradled in a floral setting fashioned from antique gold—but felt like a lead weight on her finger. It was a sham, a deceit, and for all the genuine emotion in its giving, it might as well have been a chunk of colored plastic.

Staring out across the rose-adorned loggia at Villa Rosa, towards the flat blue mirror of the swimming pool, all her girlish dreams of being presented with this, the Lisitano betrothal ring, came back to her on a dark, bitter wave.

She'd cherished those fantasies and embellished them again and again in her imagination. The basis had always been Nick, down on one knee on this very spot. Often, moonlight bathed them in magic, the scent of roses and lemons intoxicating in the air. The moment when he professed his never-ending love for her was always utterly perfect.

"Idiot!"

She curved one hand around the other and hid the ruby. Her blood seethed when she thought how mundane and non-magical the moment had actually been.

He'd just handed her the box, and when she'd fumbled and dropped the ring in the foot well of the limousine, he'd as good as tutted at her, then fielded it effortlessly and slid it onto her engagement finger with an insulting lack of ceremony, much less emotion.

It was an action for which she'd never be able to forgive him.

Reaching for her glass of chilled lemonade, her fingers made contact with the bloom of condensation and she wished could find the same degree of cool for herself. These last couple of days had been confusing and stressful, and she'd spent the entire time simmering with antipathy towards Nick.

Oh, and fighting the unwanted rip of desire every time she set eyes on him didn't help either. Ever since La Girandole and then the tussle in the limousine her erotic sense had chimed like radar in his presence.

*I don't want to want you, Nick!*

She set aside her cool drink because it wasn't lemonade she thirsted for. Grimly, she stared out across the weathered stone flags, towards the pool, seeing nothing of the shimmering water or the rambling banks of spring flowers beyond.

*And I want to love you even less, Nick, because it's pointless and futile.* She exposed the ring again, and twisted it on her finger, disturbed that it was a perfect, faultless fit.

On arriving at the clinic where Carlo was recovering, she'd not relished having to put on a bravura dramatic performance.

*One half of a blissfully engaged couple?*

Oh, please, that was the last thing she'd felt. But still it had been essential not to disappoint, disturb or upset the elder Lisitano.

Thankfully, her acting skills hadn't been taxed as much as she'd feared. A sense of shock and genuine happy surprise had carried her through what should have been a tricky ordeal. And she could still see those same emotions of incredulity and then pure joy on Nick's face as they'd been ushered into Carlo's presence. Not to mention the fugitive hint of suspicion that also passed across his beautiful carved features.

For the nurse led them not into a hushed ICU where the only sounds were the beeping of life-preserving monitors and machinery, but into a light, cheerful and frankly luxurious private room complete with television, huge banks of flowers and a commanding view of the clinic's landscaped gardens.

Carlo Lisitano was sitting up in bed wearing silk pajamas and a very elegant designer robe. He was animatedly engrossed in the football match being shown on his large screen TV, but when he caught sight of them, his brown, weathered face creased into a delighted smile.

"Anna! *Cara mia. Che bella.*" Sitting up in his bed with astonishing energy, he opened his arms and held them out to her. "Come here and let me look at you."

Her eyes flicked to Nick, noting his puckered brow and a deepening look of disbelief. They exchanged glances and he shrugged, infinitesimally.

Carlo's hug was astonishingly vigorous for a man who was supposed to be recovering slowly and with difficulty after major heart surgery. Anna returned it with caution, worried about his post-operative wound.

"Hello, *Zio Carlo*," she said as he released her. She'd always referred to him as uncle because he was so kind to her. "It's a relief to see you looking so...so well."

The older man's appearance was indeed miraculously robust. He'd lost weight since she'd last seen him, obviously, but his color was good, his eyes were bright and his thick iron-grey hair seemed to spring from his scalp with health and life.

"*Si, ragazza,*" he growled, his accent thick but his affection clear. "It's amazing what a little good news can do for a man. Eh, *figlio mio?*" He flashed a smile that was heavy with meaning at his son and then held out an arm to him too. Nick dutifully came forward to receive an enthusiastic fatherly greeting.

Anna frowned now, still twisting the ruby ring. Father and son had conversed in rapid, idiomatic Italian that she'd not been able to follow as well as she'd liked. Some phrases had sprung out, and though Nick was obviously deeply relieved to see Carlo's much improved condition, it was obvious he had suspicions about it too.

When at last the nurse had ushered them from the room, as it was time for Carlo to undergo a series of tests, Anna had expected Nick to remark on his father's condition, but instead he'd spoken only in barely more than monosyllables. Deep preoccupation was set forbiddingly across his brow, and all her attempts to engage him in conversation, about Carlo or any other topic, had been met with brief answers that had bordered on taciturnity.

*He's tricked you, hasn't he? And now you're pissed off and you're working out how quickly you can wriggle out of this ridiculous sham.*

The more time passed in Italy, the more she became convinced of this deduction. She saw little of Nick, other than when they were visiting the clinic, and the more she saw of father and son together, the plainer it became that the younger Lisitano was not pleased that he'd been deceived.

*Oh, it's okay for you to deceive others, but when someone pulls a fast one on you—even your own father—there's hell to pay.*

And yet the game went on. The charade they played out in Carlo's room at the clinic. Hands were held. Cheeks were subjected to the occasional kiss. Nick's arm would slide possessively around her. In spite of the fact that his father was clearly well on the road to recovery and would not suffer an irrevocable relapse if his son were *not* engaged, they still acted like a betrothed couple in love.

But only in public.

It was almost as if Nick had lost all desire for her since those incendiary moments in his limousine. He made no sexual overtures, and the fact that Anna had been assigned a bedroom of her own, for old-fashioned Italian propriety's sake, seemed to bother him not at all.

*What's the matter? Was I too easy?* Or was it something else? Something that made her blood run cold?

Had she somehow, through actions rather than words, revealed that she loved him? And by doing so committed the most cardinal sin of all—imply that she wanted more than just the convenient sexual relationship he'd envisioned for the duration of their fake engagement? Was that the reason why he was always elsewhere, attending to business, and not keeping her company here at Villa Rosa?

She glanced at her mobile phone where it sat on the small glass-topped table beside her lounger, wanting to ring somebody, anybody, and to pour out the real story of what was happening.

But she couldn't. She'd already rung her father several times with reports on Carlo, but it was getting harder and harder to maintain the facade for Clive and field his subtle and not so subtle questions about when "the big day" might be.

It was the same with Lydia. Although she sensed her aunt was aware that appearances might be deceiving. But Lydia was too discreet and sensitive to press and pry for the full story.

Picking up the tiny unit, she scrolled through her list of

numbers and selected Nick's. For several long moments, her fingertip hovered over "OK", wanting to press it but not knowing what she could say to him.

Part of her wanted to know the truth about what he felt for her. But another part already knew it, and was foolishly hoping that he might change. And he might get over his aversion to commitment and to love and all of a sudden say, "Let's make it real."

"You don't need to call me. I'm here."

The phone fell to the hard stone of the patio flags with an ominous clatter, but miraculously remained in one piece, the LCD still damningly showing Nick's name. The man himself reached down and swept it up, scanning the unit for damage before clearing the number and handing it back to her.

"Thank you." Her voice was small, squeezed by the sudden dryness in her mouth and throat.

Nick stood before her almost naked, an abbreviated black Speedo his only garment, and a thick white towel slung over his gleaming, gilded shoulder. Tiny shafts of stray sunlight peeped through the climbing woven greenery of the loggia and glanced off his hair, striking it pure gold like the victory coronet of some Roman god. The same light highlighted the perfection of his body.

"What were you going to call about?"

His voice was low and cautious, almost wary. Tossing his towel onto the lounger beside hers, he continued to loom over her in a challenging exhibition of his breath-catching maleness.

"I just wondered if we were going back to the clinic today, to see Carlo."

Nick's eyes narrowed. "Not today. He has more tests scheduled and he begins his physiotherapy. Remember?"

She did. She'd just said the first thing that had come into her head. But she didn't want Nick to think the aborted call would have been about *him*.

"Yes, now you mention it."

Nervously, she reached for her glass again, wishing Nick would move and not continue to stand there, menacing her with his body. The drink had lost some of its chill now but she was grateful for it. She would have drunk pond water to loosen the constriction that seemed to grip her vocal chords.

"I...I thought you'd be busy again today." She set down the glass with rattle as her hand shook uncontrollably.

"All work and no play...you know? Makes Niccolo a dull boy."

Nick's voice was softer, the note of accusation gone. He sounded almost playful suddenly, and as he hunkered down beside her lounger there was a flash of glittering light in his eyes. Without warning, he reached out and smoothed a strand of hair away from her brow, his fingertips like a streak of flame where they brushed her skin.

"Apparently, my father's spies have been telling him I'm not spending enough time with you and I've been taken to task for neglecting my fiancée."

"I'm perfectly okay on my own," Anna protested, wanting to edge away but unable to. Nick's fingers had slid to her jaw now, his thumb delicately stroking her chin, and she was paralyzed by the surge of her own hormones. "I mean...it's not as if this is a real engagement, is it?"

The gliding thumb slid across her lower lip in a slow, sensuous exploration, and like a tiny mammal transfixed by a raptor, she could not look away from his dark, compelling eyes. Fugitive emotions, questions and challenges seemed to move somewhere in their depths and, for a moment, Anna imagined the most preposterous things that he might suddenly say to her. That she longed for him to say.

The moment seemed to prolong, as if time were halted, and as the delicate pressure he was exerting increased infinitesimally, he seemed to be inviting her to take his thumb between her lips in a daring, evocative shadow-play. The suggestion of another more intimate caress.

"No," he conceded at last, withdrawing his hand, then flicking away another strand of hair from her brow, "But it has to appear real." His long, strangely dark lashes swept down, masking his eyes for a second. "And there's no reason why we shouldn't enjoy the masquerade, is there?"

Anna stiffened, then jerked away from him as his cold words in the car echoed in her head. She got as far as framing her retort, but Nick seemed to second-guess her, his face growing gentler, almost rueful.

"I know. I was an ungrateful boor," he admitted with a shrug, as if he'd read her mind and heard his own harshness read back to him. "You offered me a beautiful gift and I behaved like a pig. I should have been more appreciative." In an innately graceful movement, he slid down to sit on the stone beside her lounger, and then reached for her hand.

"But I promise to do better from now on."

Taking her trembling hand in both of his, he raised it to his lips and kissed the palm. His tongue flicked out and he licked her skin in an evocative caress of his own, as at the same time, the blue of his eyes grew hazed and sultry.

Anna gasped, her body responding as if the evocation were the actual act. Desire seemed to hurtle along her veins like a pinball, rebounding here...then here...then here...

She didn't know if Nick was telling the truth or whether he was playing some kind of game again. Maybe he was just acting his role for Carlo's spies—presumably his housekeeper, Gianna, who was a faithful and tyrannical family servant of long standing.

But Anna didn't care. The touch of Nick's tongue against her palm was electric. It made her want everything he seemed to be offering and more...and to hell with the consequences.

Her bones felt as if they were melting, and she knew that had he drawn her down onto the stone beside him, she would have surrendered her all to him and parted her legs to invite his pleasure.

Unbidden, she reached out to him and laid her fingers against his shoulder, thrilling to the satin texture of his skin and the feel of the powerful musculature beneath. Nick looked up again, his mouth still against her palm, a wealth of expression and understanding gleaming beneath the veil of his lashes.

*He knows I want him.*

The thought was fatalistic, as if some great engine had been set in motion, one that could not be braked in time to stop the inevitable.

*He knows that I'll not say no if he asks. Not even if he merely suggests...*

Nick planted one last long, slow kiss, then, in a movement as effortless and athletic as his descent, he got to his feet and urged her to rise beside him.

Bewitched, she did.

"Come, *cara mia*," he murmured, folding his hand around hers in a grip that was both gentle and commanding. "The sun's getting too hot. We should go inside."

Without waiting for her answer, he began to exert a pull, drawing her behind him as he made for the open door leading to the cooler interior of the villa.

"But wh-what about your swim?" she stammered, glancing down at his swimming trunks, and then blushing furiously at what they couldn't conceal.

"I don't want to swim," was his answer as he paused and turned to study her face, his own intent, somehow both focused but also distracted. "I only want to drown."

The words were cryptic, but Nick's meaning unequivocal.

He didn't stop in the salon. Of course, she hadn't expected him to. Instead he led her through the hall towards the wide stone steps leading to the upper level. A gentle breeze was blowing through the entire house from the open windows, making curtains everywhere flutter, but it didn't cool the heat in her blood. The heat that kept her following, following...

It was only when they reached the upper landing that she managed to hesitate before the door to her room.

Here, yes. Here would be better. Not Nick's own room, where everything that was wrong between them had been triggered four endless years ago.

But Nick shook his head, drew her onwards.

"We have demons to exorcise, *tesoro mio*," he said softly, raising the hand he'd kissed before momentarily to his lips again before guiding her on, towards his own bedroom.

And then they were there. Back in the place where it had all begun—the real, physical love, the irrational hate, the confusion and separation.

Anna felt a jolt of cold fear as the door swung closed behind them, but it was blasted away by pure heat a moment later when Nick slid down his Speedo, stepped out of it and kicked it away.

Anna gulped.

No matter how many times she saw Nick completely naked, nothing could lessen impact of his beauty.

His lean strength. The harmony of his limbs and torso. The honeyed satin gold of his skin. The primordial magnificence of his aroused maleness.

"Anna."

His voice was a husky murmur as he stepped forward and pressed his unclothed body against the entire length of her clothed one. She was only wearing shorts, a cotton vest and skimpy underwear, but the contrast between the two of them suddenly seemed breathtakingly exotic. She slid arms around him as he possessed her mouth, her fingers sliding greedily over his warm, smooth back and the tight muscularity of his buttocks. He seemed totally untroubled by the disparity between them, and as his tongue plunged and tasted, he roved his hands over her too, caressing her just as comprehensively through her clothes.

The kiss went on for many minutes, and while she felt totally absorbed in it, and in him, a part of her registered her surroundings, his room, so familiar that it was imprinted on her brain forever. Thin drapes fluttered at the windows, the flower-scented air from the garden mingling with the faint but evocative fragrance of Nick's signature cologne, which came from his own body and from the items of clothing strewn casually across an old carved high-back chair.

The bed was an antique too, its dark headboard adorned with beautifully worked images of vines and fruits. She imagined it might have been a marriage bed at one time, but she shivered with a sudden, bitter melancholy when reminded that it would never be hers.

"What's wrong, *ragazza mia*?"

The words were a caress against her mouth, soft as breath.

161

"Nothing," she whispered in return, suddenly famished for more of him. For total contact. Total possession.

"Come to bed then." He pressed kiss against her brow. "Don't be afraid." His soothing hand moved against her back and then slipped beneath her thin vest to sample the texture of her skin. At the same time he pressed his pelvis against her belly, imprinting his need on her through the fragile barrier of her shorts and panties. "It will be all right."

*But will it?*

The question tolled as Anna let herself be led forward. Nick tossed back the old embroidered coverlet and urged her down onto the pristine linen sheets beneath.

*Will it ever be all right with you if you don't really love me?*

But as he stripped off her clothes, quickly but gently, nothing mattered. Least of all that.

Four years.

It had been four years since they'd been in this room together, and yet to Nick, it seemed but a moment ago. He remembered the surprise of slowly waking to find her naked in his bed, and then the wonder, the pure wonder of her innocent but impassioned responses.

And there hadn't been a day or night since when he'd not relived that experience. Making love to her at La Girandole had been pure magic, but this, his own room, was the ambience that had haunted him. He couldn't remember a time between that first night, and this moment, right now, when he'd not wished for a chance to go back and make right what had gone so spectacularly wrong after that first sweet coupling.

Slowly, with reverence, and exerting every ounce of self-control he could muster, he began to kiss her again, lying beside her exquisite bare body, excited beyond endurance by the sight and scent of her.

He wanted to do things for her and to her that would erase all the pain that had passed between them, and also the pain he knew was surely to come. Anna was beautiful and precious. A woman meant to be worshipped for all time by a devoted lover. A devoted husband.

But he couldn't be that man, or that husband, because if he attempted it, he'd bring disaster down on both of them, just as Carlo had made his mother's life a hell.

"Nick, what is it?"

Her soft voice broke the dark spell that had momentarily gripped him and returned him to the moment. It was a moment that they must enjoy and celebrate and set in the preserving amber of their memories to be recalled and cherished later.

For now he must quench the fires that had been burning in his blood for so long.

"*Que bella...que bella,*" he murmured, laying his hand against her breast, savoring its perfect curve and the sublime softness of her skin. No other woman had skin as fine and sweet as hers, and with a groan, he lowered his head to suckle the tender bud of her nipple, glorying in her answering impassioned whimpers.

Adoring her with his mouth, he let his hands rove across her flesh, shaping the slender contours of her hips and thighs, the seductive roundness of her buttocks. She was everything a woman should be, and artlessly wonderful. The practiced, knowing, supremely self-aware skills of his former lovers slipped away into insignificance in the face of her near-innocent responses.

And yet he could sense her overwhelming desire to please

him. It was genuine. It was open. *Per Dio*, he thought, momentarily, it was loving...

He shouldn't allow that. He shouldn't encourage it, but for the moment he was helpless in the thrall of her enchantment. When he slid his fingertips between her thighs and she bucked against him, gasping and clutching at his back, his heart leapt and his sex hardened almost to agony.

She was molten. Like liquid silk that flowed and invited. Releasing her nipple, he rubbed his face against her breasts, twisting his head this way and that against their warm alabaster-smooth slopes, caressing and yet at the same time clenching his teeth in an effort to contain the rolling tide of his famished hunger for her.

*Control. Control. Not yet!* he chanted in his head, fighting to remain master of his own body so he could give pleasure, pleasure and more pleasure to hers.

But it was so difficult. He was drowning in the scents of her body. His senses were drenched by the light, fresh fragrance of her perfume and the darker and more dangerous aura of her arousal. Summoning a supreme effort of will, he curbed his body's surge and applied himself to increasing Anna's delight.

Kissing her silky throat, he circled his fingertips delicately against the very quick of her, teasing and playing with her sensitive flesh, exploring and inciting. Her cries became hoarse, almost feral, completely without inhibition—and he gloried in them.

The more raggedly she whimpered and the harder her slender body thrashed against him, the more determined he became to raise her up to the highest peak.

And suddenly, almost without warning, he felt her reach it. Arching like a bow, rigid with sensation, she uttered a high, shocked wail, and then called out his name, over and over again, like a mantra. Against his caressing fingertips he felt a deep and powerful ripple, and in some dim periphery of his mind, he experienced the pain of her fingernails digging deeply into the flesh of his back and shoulder.

After several long, timeless moments, he felt her come down, descend slowly from the high bright place and return to reality. His name was still on her lips, but it was softer now, a warm, sultry yet wondrous evocation of gratitude.

"You are beautiful, Anna," he heard himself murmur, "There's no one like you."

It was true, but it filled him with a shock of sudden foreboding. A fear...

"I could say the same about you," she replied softly, in a voice that sounded both awed and unexpectedly determined. Holding her against him, Nick had let his eyes close, to relish the moment of her climax and crystallize it somehow, but now they snapped open and he looked down into her perfect face.

It was a face full of many fleeting emotions. Some were familiar—like pure, sexual satiation. Others were more obscured, passing too quickly across her pale features for him to categorize. Disquiet gripped him. She was hiding things— even at a moment like this—but he sensed he knew what was beneath the veil and wished that he had not encouraged it. For her sake.

A second later though, analysis was blasted away, as she stirred sinuously in his arms, and then drew away from him, pushing him determinedly onto his back against the mattress.

"My turn now, *ragazzo*," she purred, the Italian endearment intoxicating on her kiss-swollen English lips, "My turn to pleasure you in return for pleasuring me."

He tried to protest, to tell her it was not necessary and that his turn would come when they joined. But she was strong, regal with a sudden female power that side-swiped him, and after one abortive attempt to rise up and embrace her, he sank back against the sheets, his heart pounding like a drum and his sex almost thudding with renewed desire.

And it was his turn to groan as she began to kiss his shoulders, his chest and finally his lower abdomen, where she nuzzled the dark-gold nest of hair that clustered there. Her soft cheek brushed his hardness and he had to clench every muscle in his body to retain control of himself.

She was a miracle. A goddess. A sorceress. And just when he thought he could bear the delicate teasing no more, she rewarded him with ultimate gift, the caress he'd been longing for, yet almost fearing.

The sweetest, silkiest heat engulfed him. The delicate flicking tongue drove him to madness. The pale sheets ripped in his tearing, gouging hands as the control he'd maintained so long began to slip...

It had been the most incredible afternoon of her life, long, golden, precious beyond measure. She would never forget it, no matter what lay ahead.

Waking from a light sleep, she felt refreshed. Both she and Nick had dozed more than once between repeated bouts of lovemaking, and he was still asleep now, stretched naked on the tangled sheets, one arm flung above his head in a beautiful attitude of complete repose.

He looked like an angel to her. But not one of those sentimental images from old-fashioned Christmas cards. Instead he was the very embodiment of a mighty warrior archangel. Powerful. Vigorous. Magnificent.

"Niccolo," she breathed, masking her own voice with a hand across her lips, reluctant to wake him after his breathtaking efforts.

As if energized by *her* passion, he'd returned to power again and again, each time lifting her to new and more unimaginable levels of bliss. He'd seemed inexhaustible, and she felt that even now, if she were but to just breathe on him, he'd wake once more and roll towards her, reaching for her body.

The temptation to reach for him in return was almost irresistible.

His skin gleamed like molten gold, and in sleep his mouth was soft and lusciously kissable. His limbs were relaxed and his sex quiescent for the moment. But she knew that it would take nothing more than the slightest hint of her interest to bring it to life again.

Roiling heat surged through her at the shock of her own boldness earlier.

It had been only the third time she'd ever made love, yet her instincts had driven her into daring. She'd taken the initiative in a way that caused her gasp, even now in the quiet aftermath.

And yet, confronted with a body as gorgeous as that of the man who lay before her, what woman who breathed could prevent herself from worshipping it?

Especially if she loved him.

*I am in so much trouble.*

Chills feathered down Anna's spine as she acknowledged the fact.

*I love him. He doesn't love me. He might not even be capable of the sort of love I want him to feel for me.*

She wished for a moment that he'd never come back into

her life, and then snatched back the wish almost immediately. These last few hours had been worth all the months of pain ahead. Perhaps years of it.

Outside, a bird began to sing in the lemon grove downhill from the villa. Its soaring cry lifted her heart. There might not be pain after all. Nick hadn't shown any signs of wanting to settle down so far, but any man could change, couldn't he? Even the most diehard of players.

For a moment she returned to the dream she'd had a few days ago. She saw herself and Nick, living together in that pink house by the Thames. With their children.

It was so seductive. So real. She looked down on him, sleeping like a temporarily vanquished god, and imagined him dreaming the same dream. Wanting the same life.

The trill of his mobile phone was like a dash of cold water thrown in her face, and the beautiful fantasy vanished.

Even as she watched Nick snap to instant, complete wakefulness, she was aware that the joyous bird out in the lemon tree had fallen silent.

"*Pronto?*"

Nick's voice was crisp. Sitting up, he raked his fingers through his tousled hair and frowned as he listened to the voice at the other end of the line. Anna couldn't make out what he was hearing, but she could tell that the conversation was in Italian. And that the person he was speaking to was in a state of high agitation. Hysteria even.

*Maria Rossi.*

As Anna listened to Nick's swift, idiomatic answers, she could make out only bits and pieces. He was trying to calm the other woman. To ascertain where she was and what she wanted. His brow crumpled as he tried to get a straight answer out of the distant Maria, then he rose to his feet and began to pace the room, heedless of his own nakedness.

*He's forgotten I'm here.* Anna felt as if she was invisible as the quick, terse Italian exchange continued. Nick's expression was intent, frowning yet clearly concerned.

*She's* the one he really cares about. I was just a convenient diversion—on hand and available because I'm part of his plans to lift his father's spirits.

Moving as quietly and unobtrusively as possible, she gathered her few clothes and slipped into them.

But as her head popped out of the neck of her vest, she finally met Nick's eyes. His frown deepened, and he put his hand over the phone.

"What are you doing?" he queried in a soft but terse voice.

"Getting dressed and getting out of here," she shot back.

What on earth did he think? That he could have his cake and eat it? Maintain an intense lover's conversation with his Italian mistress, and then return to the bed he'd just shared with his English one?

"Wait!" His eyes flashed with real irritation.

But at that moment there came the harsh, tinny sound of a protest from the mobile phone and his attention switched back to the unit, his voice quieter, more mellifluous as he replied.

Shoving her feet into her sandals, Anna almost ran for the door, heart aching. She didn't mean to look back, but she couldn't help herself.

A horrible premonition gripped her. This might be the last time—ever—that she saw Nick under such intimate circumstances, the last ever chance to see his perfect male beauty.

As she turned, he gestured to her to stay, even as he murmured soothingly into the phone. But she grabbed the door handle, turned it fumblingly and this time she did run, almost stumbling from the room, racked with pain and mortification.

# Chapter Nine

In the shower, Anna hugged herself and let the water stream down and down and down. But it didn't wash away the bitter, churning emotions.

*Maria Rossi.*

*I should have known I didn't stand a chance against her.*

Pushing her wet hair back, Anna tilted up her face as if seeking clarity in the stream from the shower.

But hadn't Nick assured her he was "just friends" with his former mistress?

"Just friends," growled Anna, reaching for the shower gel, "We all know what that means to you, Nick, don't we?"

And yet, it just didn't seem possible. It didn't seem like him at all. Yes, he was notorious as a connoisseur of glamorous women, and she accepted that he'd probably slept with a whole raft of the most stunning beauties in Europe.

But to sleep with one while still involved with another? Well, that just didn't seem like his style. It went against everything she'd ever fundamentally believed about him. Even though she'd made mistakes with respect to Nick and his actions and motives, she did believe that at core he had values and decency. He couldn't be a cheat, could he?

The thoughts turned over and over in her head as she

toweled herself dry, but she couldn't come up with an answer. Just more questions. Wrapping the large bath sheet around her body, she trudged through into her bedroom and then stopped short as her heart gave a great, hard leap.

Nick was sitting on the edge of her bed, bare-chested and barefoot, and wearing only a pair of weather-beaten old jeans. He sprang to his feet almost immediately, but dimly she registered that the instant before he'd been frowning and deep in thought.

And he was still frowning.

"Why did you run away like that?" Accusation made his eyes dark as indigo. "There was no need to."

Sudden, acid anger boiled in Anna's breast, but she controlled it carefully. No use behaving like a jealous shrew, even if he had been talking to "the other woman". She had to affect a casual aura. Keep things light. No strings. Even if her heart was ripping in two.

"You were busy. I thought we were done."

She manufactured a slight shrug, even an attempt at a nonchalant smile. But a band of fear gripped her as she watched the skin around Nick's beautiful mouth grow tight and pinched. The darkness in his eyes flashed dangerously, like thunder.

"Do you think so little of what we did together this afternoon? Do you think so little of me, that I'd dismiss you so casually after what we shared?" His hands flexed, clenched, almost as if he too were fighting negative inner urges. Ones such as the desire to grab her and shake her.

Drawing in a deep breath, she fought for as much detached dignity as she could summon whilst clad only in a towel in the presence of a man who knew every single inch of her body.

"You were talking to Maria Rossi. A *friend* of yours. I was

172

obviously surplus to requirements."

The moment the words were out of her mouth, she wished them back again. She'd said exactly the sort of thing she'd told herself she wouldn't sink to, and every fabulous line of Nick's body seemed to vibrate with anger.

"I'm afraid you're mistaken, Anna."

His coolness was far more ominous than any amount of sound and fury, and the sound of her name, heavy with emphasis, made the words doubly cutting.

"I'm an Italian. This is Italy. Do you seriously believe she's the only person I'm likely to talk on the phone to in my native language?" He turned away and stalked towards the open window. The hard, taut line of his bare back told her that he saw nothing of the colorful, landscaped gardens that lay beyond.

"For all you know I could have been speaking to my father's nurse...or to his doctor."

Abject horror made Anna feel suddenly sick. What the hell was the matter with her? How could she have thought the worst of him? Even more horrible, what was the matter with Carlo? And yet the tone... You didn't talk to a composed medical professional that way, did you?

"I'm sorry," she said, keeping her voice low as if that might stop her from saying anything else stupid, "Is Carlo all right? There hasn't been some setback, has there?"

Nick spun around. "Well, thank you for enquiring at last."

His voice was low too, and cutting, and yet a strange look of confusion and sorrow passed fleetingly across his face. It so reminded Anna of the maelstrom of her own feelings that for a second she wanted to shoot across the room and console him with a hug.

But then he went on, tensely, "No, as a matter of fact, my father is fine. Still improving. I've just spoken to him."

"Then who *were* you talking to?" she asked, grasping the bull by the horns. Better to know for certain, deal with it and stop driving herself crazy.

Nick's shoulders suddenly dropped, and for a moment he looked defeated, and infinitely weary.

"To Letti, Maria's PA." His voice was flat now, and the impression of tiredness intensified. "There's been an accident. Maria's smashed up her car, and she's injured and she's asking for me. I'm afraid I've got to go back to England straight away." He gave her a level look. "That's what I was speaking to Carlo about. The jet's being prepared. You're welcome to stay on here if you like. You could have a little holiday, maybe?" His eyes narrowed oddly, as if gauging her somehow. "But if you want to return to London, I'd be grateful if you'd start packing straight away."

Another wave of pain and confusion washed through her, with a breaker of self-loathing crashing in behind. Her heart was screaming because the beauty of what she and Nick had shared was being snatched away from her. And at the same time, she hated herself for resenting a woman who was hurt, possibly seriously.

*Don't be such a selfish cow, Anna.*

Furiously, she smashed down the remnants of her self-pity, and her anger at the capricious way fate seemed to persist in punishing her for going to bed with Nick. She *must* get over herself, and do what was right. The opportunity to wail and rail and lick her wounds would have to be postponed to some private and very secret time.

"How...how is Maria? Is it very serious?" She kept her voice calm. Tried to put herself in Nick's place and imagine hearing that a woman he'd been very close to, and may *still* be close to, had been injured.

"I'm not sure. I couldn't get much sense out of Letti." He shrugged; looking worried as his broad, gleaming shoulders lifted. "She isn't exactly the calmest and most level of women. Which is exactly why someone with a cooler head should be there to look out for Maria's interests. Film people are notoriously superficial and prone to making bad decisions."

He was right.

"Yes, you need to be there," Anna said quietly. Her emotions felt deadened and numb. She struggled to feel what she knew was right and appropriate, but it suddenly seemed as if she'd been turned into a robot.

"Are you coming to London with me?"

Nick too sounded oddly mechanical, so different from the fiery, passionate, magical man she'd lain entwined with earlier.

"Yes. Yes, I'll come," she replied, wishing him out of the room suddenly so she could dress. Pack. Tentatively attempt to feel something, or at least see if she could bear to feel it. "Unless you think I should stay and visit Carlo a bit more?"

Nick's beautiful mouth thinned, and he spoke with a shocking, unexpected vehemence.

"I think my sainted father will do very well indeed without the presence of either of us, *cara*. He was doing perfectly fine, it seemed, before we arrived. *And* before that, so I'm now—finally—informed."

"What do you mean?" Anna's stomach began to sink again. She felt rather odd.

"I mean that I—or should I say *we* have been deceived. Carlo was never quite as ill in his post-operative phase as I've been led to believe. He is an accomplished actor, and skilled at coaxing others to..." Again, that exquisite, expressive shrug. "Well, not exactly lie on his behalf, but to be flexible with the truth."

She was aware that her mouth was hanging open foolishly. What was he trying to say?

Nick went on, striding back towards her. "Yes, he convinced me that he was in a decline and that the only thing that would halt it would be news of our engagement. Now it seems he was recovering normally, and simply saw an opportunity to get what he wanted...and took it."

Anna could no longer look at him. She glanced down at her hands and the beautiful ring she saw on her left one felt as heavy as a lead ingot. But when she started to tug at it, Nick reached out and clasped her hands, preventing her from pulling off the empty symbol of nothingness.

"Perhaps we should maintain the fiction for a little while longer," he said evenly. "My father is considerably more recovered than I believed him to be. But even so, a sudden disappointment isn't going to do him any good at this critical stage."

"Of course," Anna concurred.

Her hands felt limp and nerveless, and they flopped to her sides when Nick released her, as if weighed down by the falseness and lack of meaning in the exquisite jewel that graced her engagement finger. "Now, if you'd just leave, I can get dressed and pack my bag. That jet's waiting, and the sooner we get home, the sooner you can get to Maria and the sooner I can get back to my work. It must be piling up and it's not fair on Lydia to leave her dealing with everything longer than necessary."

For a moment, it seemed as if Nick was going to say something—a wealth of indecipherable emotion seemed to pass behind those glittering blue eyes—but instead he merely nodded and walked swiftly from the room. He was every bit the high-flying decision-maker now, even though his feet were bare and he wore just the oldest pair of jeans.

It was only when the door was closed firmly behind him that Anna sank to her knees, hands covering her face as she tried to hold in the tears.


The return to London in the Learjet felt like being enclosed in a strange bubble of limbo, a timeout from one crisis before he had to face the next.

Just as before, Anna kept her nose firmly in a magazine, but as Nick watched her, he observed a tension in her limbs that matched his own. It was agony not to tap his foot or his fingers to relieve it. The deeply upholstered seat felt about as comfortable as a pile of rocks.

He hated himself.

It was an effort to force his mind back to Maria and the car smash. He knew he should be planning strategies to ensure she received the best care and achieved the quickest recovery. Trying to find ways to ensure that it didn't happen again and that she remained free of the addictions that he had no doubt had caused her accident.

And yet his mind and his heart wouldn't obey him. His thoughts, his very consciousness kept circling around, and focusing on the woman who was sitting a few feet away.

He'd hurt her again. Badly.

*I'm poison for you, Anna*, he told her silently. *I'm just as venomous as my father was to my mother.* A great weight seemed to settle in his chest, making it hard to breathe, and he knew that his scheme to cheer up Carlo had been a horrific misfire.

He should never have come near Anna again, for her sake. He should have known that the instant he was back in her company, he'd want her again. His mouth thinned in self-disgust. His own special pleading appalled him.

*Get her out of my system? Give us both some fun during the masquerade? Stronzate!* He'd simply indulged his appetites, and now she—an innocent and loving young woman—was paying the price.

And yet...

Horrified, he felt his body rousing again as his wayward imagination swept him back to those hours in his bedroom at Villa Rosa. Lovemaking had never been so perfect, so deep and so complete. So rich with emotion.

The last thought filled him with dread.

*No!* He couldn't allow those feelings. Not now. Not ever. He was his father's son and he could never allow himself to love, because to love would be to destroy the one he loved.

He had to nip everything in the bud right now. His feelings. Her feelings. Stop now, before they were sucked in deeper and did something stupid that would only bring greater agony further down the road. Look what had happened to vulnerable Maria when the two of them had become involved. The thought that Anna too might be at risk from him was so intolerable that it made his gut clench in actual nausea.

But suddenly, because he was in the grip of something he'd never expected to feel, he knew exactly how to end it. He'd try the tactic that had worked so well before.

Anna looked up from the copy of Elle International that she

hadn't read a word of and found Nick's eyes upon her. His look was intense, almost calculating, and she wondered how she could ever have thought—while she was in his arms—that she'd seen all his barriers melting and falling down.

*You're an idiot, girl.* She attempted to flash him a calm, amenable smile, yet knew it would appear as brittle and false as those of the models in her magazine. *He'll never have the feelings you projected upon him then. It's not in his nature.*

Okay, so maybe Nick could feel affection as well as lust for the women who tumbled into his bed, but it was only for that moment. It was transitory, and he was probably fooling himself as much as he was fooling his paramours.

But as for the longer term? Well, he'd told her himself that commitment just wasn't his style, so why had she ever begun to entertain ideas that he might change?

Because that was what she'd been doing, wasn't it? Imagining that one of these days, either in bed with him or out of it, he was going to turn to her and say "let's make it all real."

Unable to bear the weight of his stare any longer, she spoke up.

"Okay, spit it out. You've obviously got something to say. And I've a feeling I'm not going to like it."

The words came out harsher than she'd wanted them to, and once again, she was furious with herself. He probably wasn't thinking about her at all. He was probably worried sick about Maria and had just happened to be looking in her direction. Oh why did this horrible emotional hotbed have the power to turn her into a cast-iron bitch?

"I'm sorry," she apologized, "I didn't meant to say that. It's just that you were looking at me very intensely. And it makes me nervous."

Nick put aside one of his ever-present files of business

papers and leant towards her slightly. He was still casually dressed, in dark jeans and a close-fitting black T-shirt, and the very somberness of his clothing made him even more intimidating. She was right, she realized. Whatever he was about to say was something she wasn't going to like.

Nick's voice was soft when the words came, but strangely precise.

"I think we've made a mistake again, Anna, don't you?"

It was exactly what she'd half been expecting, but it still hit her like a punch to the solar plexus. The statement—in that cool, manufactured tone—was so similar to one spoken four years ago, that she had to fight not to show that it had knocked the wind out of her.

She dragged in a breath, willing her prickling eyes not to well over. She *must* not show how much this was killing her. She must remain calm, apparently unconcerned. It wouldn't make it hurt any less than last time, but at least this time she'd still have her pride and he wouldn't know how much she was shriveling up inside.

"I was wondering when that would come," she said, stiffening her spine, bracing her shoulders and fabricating what she hoped looked like a wry smile.

Nick blinked, his dark lashes flashing down, and Anna swore that for split second she saw admiration in the blue depths of her eyes. *He knows I'm kidding him,* she thought, battling to maintain her feigned nonchalance. *Well, I'm just going to have to try harder.*

"In fact, I've been thinking of saying the very same thing myself." She paused, thinking fast and on the fly, not wanting to make a mistake. "We both know it's messy to mix pleasure with business. And that's all this engagement thing has been, really, isn't it? Just a deal between us. A convenient arrangement. Mutually beneficial."

Nick was frowning now, his brilliant eyes narrowing.

"I help you," she rushed on, the words not as crisp and businesslike as she would have preferred, "And you, hopefully, help Dad out of a tight spot." She swallowed, hoping she'd not been too explicit. "I mean, that was part of the subtext, wasn't it?"

The beautiful mouth that she'd kissed so desperately became a hard, tight line. "Why won't you believe me? It really was always my intention to provide refinancing for Felgate's. Your helping me was *never* a condition, Anna. I would have done it even if you'd said no."

She watched as he rubbed the palm of one hand with the thumb of the other. It was an uncharacteristically revealing gesture, and she wondered if he was aware of what he was doing. Nick was normally the master of poker-faced opacity.

"Oh," she said, feeling small. In this at least, she knew she should have trusted him. "Well, in that case I'm sorry—again—that I mistrusted you."

"I thought you agreed to help me because you really cared about Carlo?"

"I do care about Carlo. Of course, I do."

"But not about me."

How could she answer that? What response could she possibly give that wouldn't reveal her? Four years ago, she'd given him her virginity and he'd unwittingly taken her heart forever. But he must never know that. She wondered how long she could stall without giving herself away.

"I'm fond of you, Nick," she said, striving for lightness, for an adult rationality. "I always have been, despite our...our differences." She looked away, unable to face his eyes. "And we're good together sexually, that's obvious." That was the greatest understatement that she, or anybody, could have perpetrated, and it tasted like ashes on her lips. "But let's face it, we're not really all that good for each other otherwise, are we?"

She risked the swiftest glance and the look of shock written across Nick's elegant male features rocked her in her seat.

Shock of her own forced her onwards. "Well, I'm right, aren't I?"

In an uncanny, almost unnerving transformation, Nick's face almost instantly became as blank and unrevealing as a sheet of polished stone.

"You are indeed," he said softly, a note in his voice that might have been menace. Or might have been something else entirely. "And I suggest, on our return to London, that we see each other as little as possible. I shall have to make arrangements for Maria's care, and probably for her return to Italy, but I think your father, and others, can be told that unfortunately I'll be travelling on business for the foreseeable future. I can certainly make that the truth."

"Well, it seems as if you've got it all worked out," Anna whipped back, stung by the clinical quality of his...his projections.

"I've given it some thought."

He sat back in his chair, his muscular arms crossed in an action that might have been construed as defensive in a man less strong and completely sure of himself. "And perhaps you could concentrate on developing Traditional Temps? You have an excellent prospect there. You've found a niche market that's viable even in times of financial uncertainty. I'd be prepared to provide a substantial investment to enable an expansion. There's certainly scope for it."

He lifted one hand, tapped a finger against his lips. She could almost see the cogs of his analytical mind turning. Assessing. Scheming. It was impossible to believe this was the same man who'd groaned her name as he'd reached the pinnacle of pleasure inside her body. "That way we could still appear to be a modern engaged couple for a while. Each continuing to pursue our separate business interests."

"I don't want a payoff," she cried, appalled.

Nick's eyes hardened like blue ice. "Not a payoff. An interest-free loan." He enunciated every syllable as if he'd been turned into a machine. "It would simply add veracity to our position."

She wanted to protest. She wanted to fly at him and slap him, shake him out of the frigid shell he'd so rapidly sealed around himself. Wasn't there even a spark of the warm, fiery, generous man who'd given himself to her so splendidly during that long, perfumed afternoon they'd shared only hours ago?

It seemed not. And the effort of fighting for something that had probably been no more than a convenient illusion suddenly seemed unbearably wearying. She sighed and looked away, out of the cabin window, into the night.

"As you wish. That sounds excellent. Thank you," she murmured.

A tiny green bud of hope that she'd barely been aware of nurturing had just been utterly and irrevocably crushed.


On their arrival in London, Nick had been coolly solicitous, arranging a separate car for Anna to take her home while he went straight to the hospital where Maria was. He'd even asked—several times—if she was all right.

His kiss on her cheek as they'd parted had been the purest, most exquisite torture. She doubted if she'd ever be all right again in her life.

*Such empty words*, she thought a couple of weeks later.

*All right?*

Probably the most meaningless expression in the world, but she'd been using it in answer to every query about her welfare since.

Acting the part of a contented fiancée parted from her fiancé purely by circumstances demanded quite a bravura performance from her, but at least she could take some small satisfaction from the fact that she kept rising to the occasion.

Queries from her father and from Lydia were searching, the latter more so. Perilously so. But eventually, even they stopped asking, although Lydia's sharp eyes continued to observe her acutely, and her aunt was especially kind and thoughtful towards her.

Anna had not seen Nick since they'd parted stiffly at the airport, but she had received a number of brief, efficient text messages from him about the proposed venture capital for Traditional Temps. The temptation to just ignore them was enormous, but she'd steeled herself to reply with just as much detachment and focus on purely practical matters. It was the only way to handle things. Anything else, any slight deviation into the realm of emotions and memories was likely to see her crumple and fall apart.

And that she could not and would not do.

She looked up from the paperwork on her desk. At least the business was doing all right. More than all right. The plans to expand and open a new office in Manchester were exciting, and she looked forward to throwing herself into them and building on what she and Lydia had already achieved. All she had to do was to remember, always, to name their new business partner as Industria Lisitano.

Always the company. Never the man. Never the man.

But when Lydia appeared in the doorway a cold, cold hand gripped her heart. Something in the look on her aunt's dear, rounded face chilled her to the bone. The other woman grimaced, shrugged and sighed. Then she placed a magazine— one of the celebrity glossies that Anna had been studiously ignoring for the last fortnight—on top of the development plans.

"I know you're going to see this sooner rather than later, love." Lyd's voice was soft and palliative, as if she were talking to a dangerously fragile invalid. "Better now, than get a shock at some news-stand or other."

She flipped open the magazine.

Somehow, Anna wasn't surprised. Not at all. A rather grainy photograph showed Maria Rossi in a wheelchair, being wheeled through an airport. At her side was Nick, and she was clutching his hand.

It appeared pretty obvious that they were back together again, and as she read the small amount of accompanying text, which admittedly consisted mostly of supposition, Anna found herself twisting the ruby ring on her finger.

She wanted it off. It was meaningless. She'd been living in limbo land for the past two weeks, but now she wanted to be out in the real world, no matter how painful it was. Free, in a world where she no longer had any connection to Nick—no matter how tenuous or contrived.

There was no way Carlo would know that she'd taken the ring off, she decided, struggling with the wretched thing. He'd be safe in his illusion for a little while longer, until he was completely out of danger.

*But if I continue to harbor illusions they'll destroy me*

185

*eventually.*

She twisted at the stuck ring, hurting her finger in a futile attempt to divert focus from the huge pain in her heart.

"Leave it," Lydia said gently, "Try it later with some hand cream."

Ignoring her, Anna braced her hand on the desk and wrenched at the ring. And as it came off, the force of releasing it ripped the open magazine page from top to bottom.

The picture of Nick's face was torn in two. And as she looked down on that image of beauty crumpled and sundered, for the first time in two weeks, she began to cry again, feeling Lydia's arm encircle her shoulder as she curled in on herself, cradling her sorrow.

# Chapter Ten

Returning to the office after meeting a prospective client, Anna shuddered when she saw a copy of UK Celeb on their new admin assistant's desk.

For six weeks, she hadn't looked at a single copy of this magazine, or any of the many similar celebrity publications. The last time she'd looked at one, or had it shown to her, she'd fallen apart, and she was determined never to let that happen again. No way.

"Help yourself," said Sandy cheerily, returning from the coffee room, "I've finished with it. There's nothing much of interest in there anyway."

"Thanks, I'll pass." Anna returned the pleasant young woman's smile, a mix of curiosity, confusion and apprehension rippling through her. Sandy would certainly have mentioned if there'd been a photo or article about her boss's fiancé featured in those garish pages.

Automatically, she twisted the ring on her left hand. She'd put it back on again. Even though communications between her and Nick continued to be to-the-point texts or emails about business or Carlo, there'd been nothing about ending their faux engagement.

"Any messages?" she enquired, moving to her desk and grimacing at the pile of new CVs she had to go through.

Flinging herself headlong into work had been mercifully therapeutic, but there were times when she wished it was safe for her to just ease off a little bit.

"Oh, yes, sorry. There was a call from *Signor* Lisitano's personal assistant. He'd like you to meet him at the Savoy, if you can." Sandy glanced at the wall clock. "For afternoon tea, around three if possible? Shall I call to confirm?"

If her admin assistant had vaulted across the desk and slapped her in the face, Anna couldn't have been more surprised and thrown into turmoil. All these weeks with nothing more than the sketchiest of contact and now this.

A summons to the Savoy.

She wondered if Sandy could actually see her heart pounding in her chest. The urge to put both hands over it in an attempt to calm its sudden, frantic leaping was almost irresistible.

Instead, she said, "Yes, please do." Her voice came out sounding surprisingly normal considering. She'd half expected to hear a strangled, nervous squawk. "I think I'd better spruce myself up a bit before I set off though, don't you?" She flashed a smile—that felt as if it were nearly cracking her face—at the friendly young woman. "The Savoy is so posh. I don't want them to have to sling me out for looking like a gypsy."

On entering the famous foyer of the Savoy, she didn't feel so much like a gypsy as someone whose entire physical constitution was about to capsize.

Nick.

Oh, how she wanted to see him. How she feared the very same thing because this might mean the end of their engagement and that their flimsy masquerade was finally over. It was a meaningless and empty relationship, but it was still a link to him.

She scanned the spacious room that was filled with happy, glamorous people enjoying the traditional English tea ceremony. Light from the chandeliers glinted off the silverware and the china, and the sound of voices seemed to rebound off the mirrored walls and double in volume.

But Anna was waiting for the sound of one familiar, deep and thrilling voice raised in greeting. Waiting for the sight of one unforgettable face, one head of shining burnished dark gold hair.

But there was neither. Instead, and to both her surprise and guilty disappointment, she saw another familiar figure rise from his seat and heard a different Italian voice say, *"Ehi! Ragazza mia! Buonasera!"*

Signor Lisitano.

Signor *Carlo* Lisitano walked towards her to greet her, enfolding her in the sort of enthusiastic hug that she doubted she would ever receive again from his absent son.

*He looks well. In fact, he looks fabulous*, she thought as they exchanged more greetings and Carlo led her to his table and got her settled. The elder Lisitano's every move was vital and energetic, and his weather-beaten face seemed to glow with a health that seemed all the more robust for having been so recently threatened. She hated herself for wishing his son was here in his place.

"You look amazing, *Zio Carlo*," she said once tea had been ordered. "How are you feeling now? You certainly look much better than you did when I last saw you."

"I feel very well, *cara*," answered Carlo, beaming. His voice was heavily accented, but his English was excellent. Almost as accomplished as his son's perfect idiomatic command of the language. "My doctors have given me a clean bill of health now

189

and proclaimed my recovery to be remarkable. Of course, I have to make certain concessions," he went on, casting a brief but longing glance at the cream cakes being served at the next table. "But even so, it is a small price to pay for being brought back to life."

Carlo's eyes were darker than those of his son and brown instead of blue, but they still had the same razor sharp perception. And they narrowed now, focusing disturbingly on her face.

"And how about you, *piccolina*?" he enquired more softly. "You are more beautiful than ever, Anna, but you are too skinny. And there are shadows beneath your eyes." He frowned momentarily, concern gathering on his impressive brow. "Which I expect is the fault of my foolish *idiota* of a son, no doubt, and of me too, alas. We shall have to do something about this, and do it quickly, don't you think?"

She didn't know what to say, and to her horror, she felt sorrow rise in her throat like a physical obstruction. And tears that she'd suppressed too long prickle dangerously in her eyes. A sob gathered, but before she could suppress it, Carlo had slid along the banquette they were sharing and she was enfolded again in a very loving and avuncular hug.

"Don't worry, *cara*," Carlo said gently, "I have spoken at length with Niccolo over the last few days, and I know what has transpired between you. I am to blame for much of it. Much more, I fear, than he is. But he is his own man, Anna, and even though we've talked as never before, he still keeps his own counsel in some things. I can only hope that the truths I have told him will allow him to see a truth of his own."

"I don't understand," she said as their tea arrived, and elder Lisitano released her and set about solicitously pouring her a cup of Earl Grey and encouraging her to eat. The sandwiches and cakes looked sumptuous, but she knew that they would probably taste like mud in her mouth until she knew what Carlo was talking about. Maybe even afterwards too.

But the fragrant tea itself was both refreshing and reviving, and she sipped it gratefully as Nick's father began a slow, careful narrative which seemed to test his excellent English to the limit.

"You don't remember my wife very much, do you, Anna?" he began, grimacing and setting aside his cup of weak tea.

"No, I don't. She died when I was tiny. I only really know her from Nick's stories about her, although I must have met her, because I remember she was lovely. But I can't recall her very clearly."

"I loved her," Carlo said simply, a wistful expression creasing his bronzed face. "I loved her with all my heart. But it was a stormy love. Fiery and full of argument. Rosa had her own fires, and she gave as good as she got much of the time. But she had hidden vulnerabilities too, and I hurt her very grievously. Much as Niccolo hurts you now."

The older man paused, and unashamedly took out a snowy white handkerchief and wiped his eyes. "And there were other faults on my part. I wasn't the man that my son is. I was weak. There were other women. Women who were easier, less emotionally intense than my sweet Rosa, and I enjoyed them." He drew in a gusty breath, "And eventually this all became too much for her...and...and—"

This time it was Anna's turn to comfort. She knew the story of Nick's mother's suicide, and she knew how deeply it had affected him. But she'd never been fully aware of its effect on Carlo too.

"Niccolo blames me for her death, and rightly so." The Italian man's voice was stronger now, as if he'd come to terms with his guilt and had accepted it. "But it has colored his own feelings more than he knows. He is wary of relationships. He distrusts love. He believes that because his mother's love for me damaged her, any woman who loves him will suffer just as much."

Dark brown eyes held hers. "And he shuns commitment for that reason. He denies love in order to protect the women he cares about. He believes he is his father's son and will blight the life of any woman he marries."

Could that be it?

Anna felt a surge of excitement and of hope. But immediately she crushed it down. Carlo had said that Nick kept his own counsel, and the reason for that was that the woman he feared he'd hurt by marrying her was probably Maria Rossi, not her. He was probably still trying to protect his father's dreams by playing down his deep commitment to the Italian actress when he knew that Carlo wanted a Lisitano and Felgate union.

She was grasping around for something to say when Carlo reached out and clasped her hand.

"But my son is a better man than I, Anna. Stronger, more intelligent and more honorable. With the right woman—" his weathered hand gripped her paler one tighter "—he will be a fine husband. A loving husband. A husband who will make a marriage that will endure indefinitely and be a source of the deepest joy for both parties."

*Yes, for Nick and Maria*, thought Anna sorrowfully. She opened her mouth, wondering how she could tell Carlo as kindly as she could that the dreams he—and her own father—obviously still harbored just couldn't come true.

But before she could speak, Carlo was looking beyond her, his face suddenly wreathed in smiles, his eyes lighting proudly.

"*Figlio mio!*" he cried, giving her hand a last squeeze before rising to his feet, stepping around the table and moving forward to hug the tall, golden-haired figure who had just appeared in the periphery of Anna's vision.

As father and son embraced, she was grateful for a moment's grace to gather her wits and keep from falling to pieces. The impact of Nick, here in the flesh instead of just the painful phantom who'd haunted her waking and sleeping dreams for the last six weeks, literally took her breath away. She fought not to gasp, not to whoosh in air like an Olympic swimmer.

How could a man she believed was perfect already manage to look even more arresting, even more male?

Clad in one of his sublimely tailored near-black suits, worn with a toning shirt and tie, Nick looked like every inch her nemesis, an avenging dark angel. He'd had his glorious hair cut recently, she noted, feeling strangely out of it, and yet at the same time able to quantify everything about him. It was much shorter, almost severe, and vaguely militaristic. And his face too, had a new harshness about it. She wasn't the only one who appeared to have lost weight.

The carved lines of Nick's classical features looked even more sculpted now. His cheekbones were sharp and the contour of his jaw hard and unforgiving.

And his eyes, when he brought them to bear upon her, drilled like lasers.

Anna's heart beat like a trip-hammer.

What's happened to him? What has he been through? Deep, deep inside her, a microscopic plume of hope blossomed, but she squashed it ruthlessly. It wasn't her he'd been suffering over, but the injured Maria—the woman he'd chosen to spend his time with instead of his fake fiancée.

As Carlo slapped his son's arm, then resumed his seat, she had absolutely no idea what to do. She was a social being. She ran her own business. She hosted her father's parties. She *always* knew what to do.

But not now. Now, she remained frozen in her seat, pinned there by the burning intensity in Nick Lisitano's bright blue gaze.

"Anna," he murmured. His voice sounded odd, and he seemed so focused on her that she could almost imagine that he'd instantly forgotten the presence of his own father. The heart that had raced and leapt in Anna's breast seemed to falter and freeze momentarily, and she couldn't help but drag in that huge breath again as he took a step towards her.

Yet still she couldn't rise. Couldn't move. Couldn't make any gesture of greeting.

But she didn't need to. Two long, beautiful hands reached down and settled one on either side of her hot face as he inclined his lean body towards her and brought his lips ever so gently down on hers.

Her heart began to thunder again, and for the second time in as many minutes, the threat that she might cry pricked acutely at her eyes.

His lips lingered, soft as velvet, yet firm and thrillingly positive upon hers. Her own mouth grew malleable, accepting. Her lips opened like a hungry flower greedy for the sun.

For a moment, an hour, a lifetime, she felt the caress of his sublimely sensual mouth upon hers, and the tantalizing touch of his tongue as it acknowledged her own yielding. Then the contact was gone and it was as if her soul went with it.

Her eyelids swept down, as if unwilling to allow him to see the totality of her emotions.

*That wasn't for you,* she told herself starkly. *That was for*

*Carlo's benefit. He still believes there's something viable between you and Nick, and Nick doesn't want to disappoint him.*

"I've missed you, *cara.*"

His voice sounded so sincere, so very real in its emotion, and his fingertips trailed across her cheek as he withdrew.

When she opened her eyes, she realized that Carlo had withdrawn to a chair at the other side of the low table, and something inside her lurched as Nick took his father's place on the banquette beside her. The light, yet stirring spice of his subtle exotic cologne made her head feel as if she were on a merry-go-round—and it whirled faster when he took her hand in his.

*It's for show. It's for show,* she repeated to herself, and yet something about the enclosing contact of his long fingers filled her with a sensation of electricity. The way he held her felt real and true. Dangerously and temptingly lasting.

For the next fifteen minutes father and son engaged in a relaxed, comfortable conversation that she knew she would never remember afterwards. It was light, social, inconsequential, and even though she participated she was barely aware of what she was saying. Every one of her senses was so completely tuned in on the heat of his hand around hers, the low, thrilling cadence of his voice, and the unearthly blue glint of his eyes every time he looked her way that she unconsciously tuned out everything else.

*He's everything I'll ever want,* she thought detachedly. *And this might be the most I'll ever have. So I'll remember every last detail about him now, even if it kills me.*

But, presently, she was forced to reconnect with sudden reality.

"I'm afraid I will have to drag Anna away from you now, Papà," Nick was saying, and as he spoke, he rose to his feet.

195

The pressure on her fingers tightened, growing momentarily imperious.

He wanted her to go with him. But where?

"So soon?" The look in Carlo's eyes belied the disappointment in his voice. It was obvious that he wanted the two of them to be alone together.

"Yes, alas...there's something I'm anxious to show her, and it involves a drive. You don't mind, do you?"

He was asking Carlo, but it also seemed as if he was asking her too. Unable to do anything other than comply, she too rose to her feet. A strange look of relief flashed briefly across his face, and then he was bidding a warm *arrivaderci* to his father.

Anna took the chance to excuse herself for a moment and retreat to the powder room.

*What does he want? Where does he want to take me? And why?*

Heat, the unpleasant, rising flush of panic, surged through her. Had she just been quietly fooling herself all these weeks that there could still possibly be something between them? It seemed she had. And now crunch time had come, along with the inevitable elucidation that he and Maria were an item again. Something Anna wasn't sure she was able to face.

*Shape up!* she ordered, looking up from where she was running cold water over her wrists to calm her frazzled nerves. *Six weeks ago you'd totally given up on him, so what's the difference now?*

Admittedly, she no longer had her relationship with Martin, but that had never really been right, and it was probably far better for both her and her erstwhile boyfriend that they'd parted. She'd heard on the grapevine that Martin was on the point of getting engaged to a new girl, one his mother absolutely doted on, and she was genuinely happy for him and knew he was better off without her.

*But where does that leave me?* She had no answers as she left the powder room and returned to the foyer.

Her heart did a somersault again at the sight of Nick standing by the door waiting for her. He was so beautiful and dramatic in the elegant dark clothing that contrasted so stunningly with his gleaming, newly short hair. Even in the few moments it took her to reach him she saw a whole series of women check him out hungrily as they entered or left the hotel.

"Ready?" he enquired lightly, his face totally unrevealing.

Anna nodded, her heart still turning over so much she was quite unable to speak. Her crooked smile felt as if it was pinned to her face as she exited in front of him through the large revolving door.

Once outside, she expected the doorman to snag them a taxi, but instead, there was a familiar throaty roar and the Vampiro slid to a halt in front of them, driven by one of the hotel's parking valets. In spite of her nervousness, Anna was amused by the awed expression on the young man's face as he stepped from the stunning black vehicle and handed it over to its owner. But she felt a moment of apprehension herself as Nick assisted her into the car. This time she was wearing a slim skirt and the Vampiro was curb-huggingly low.

"Where are we going?" she asked once they were underway and Nick was expertly threading his way through the city's afternoon traffic.

"You'll see," he answered neutrally, slanting her a momentary sideways glance before returning his full attention to the stream of vehicles jockeying around the Vampiro. "It won't take too long," he added, the cryptic note in his voice also seeming to suggest that they keep the conversation to a minimum.

*Fine by me*, she thought, admitting now she was finally alone with him she didn't actually know what to say. Their situation was so weird, so badly defined. They were still acting as if they were engaged, obviously, for Carlo's sake. But in reality, had they broken up the last time they'd seen each other? It seemed that way, but nothing had been said. Nothing had really been agreed.

Suddenly weary, she let her head sink back against the deeply padded headrest and tried to clear her mind of all thoughts and fears and worries.

Astonishingly, after a few moments of listening to traffic noise, she seemed to achieve her goal. Not even Nick blowing the Vampiro's horn, and muttering something dark sounding in Italian as another motorist cut him up, could disturb her. Against the odds, she drifted into a shallow sleep.

It occurred to her, just as her consciousness began to fuzz, that it was because six long weeks of tension and speculation were finally almost over. Wherever they were going, she'd soon know for certain if it was genuinely the end with Nick.

Once they were clear of Central London and on a quieter road well on their way to their destination, Nick finally allowed himself the luxury of glancing at the woman asleep beside him.

His heart clenched at the sight of Anna's beautiful face, and guilt washed over him as he recognized the refining effect of weight-loss and the faintest of delicate violet shadows beneath her eyes.

They were his fault. They were the product of pain caused by him. He drew in a ragged breath, swearing with every fiber of his heart and soul and body that he would wipe away those signs of unhappiness and tension and replace them with a glow of contentment, peace and security.

If she would allow him, he'd keep her from sadness for as long as she lived.

Anna came awake with a jolt, alerted by a sharp beeping sound and aware that the powerful car had slowed to a crawl. She rubbed her eyes carefully, instinctively remembering that she was wearing her everyday business makeup and that it wouldn't do to look like a startled panda in front of Nick. Even if she felt like one.

Blinking, she studied their surroundings, her heart thudding with a sudden, almost fatalistic surprise when she saw that they were sliding between the open gates of the distinctive pink house they'd happened upon all those weeks ago. The night that they'd visited La Girandole and made love for the very first time in four long years.

"What are we doing here?"

Struggling with her seatbelt, she glanced from the rosy facade of the quirky rambling building to Nick's intent face beside her. He wasn't looking at the pretty pink house, but at her face, his blue eyes burningly intense and as watchful as a hawk's. Pocketing the tiny remote that had opened the gates for them, he reached over and deftly, and without looking what he was doing, he released her from the harness. His attention remained completely focused on her.

About to repeat her question, she froze to stillness when he reached out and forestalled her words with the lightest touch of his fingertip on her lips.

"Hush, *ragazza*," he murmured, and then a moment later, he was out of the car, around to her side, and had the Vampiro's dramatic gull-wing door lifting open.

Taking her hand, he helped her out on to the raked gravel drive. Gently, but brooking no protest, he led her towards the dark gleaming burgundy-painted door to the house. As they stood on the threshold, he extracted a key from his pocket and let them in, quickly deactivating a security alarm set on the wall, just within.

"How did you do that? What are we doing here? Who owns this place?"

Anna's eyes darted to and fro, noting the spacious, low-ceilinged entrance hall that still exuded a friendly air of being lived in and loved even though it appeared to be almost entirely bereft of furniture. The walls were painted a mellow honeyed peach above half-paneling in some warm and polished wood.

"Questions. Questions. Questions." Nick's voice now bore a note of amusement as he locked the door and pocketed the key, before taking her hand again and drawing her closer to him.

"*I* own this place," he said, looking down into her eyes.

"Oh," was all Anna could manage, transfixed by the sight of his beautiful mouth just inches above her own. Insane thoughts, fantasies and hopes began to racket around inside her. They threatened to get out of control, and she fought, desperately and ruthlessly, to splat them down.

*Don't hope!* she commanded herself. *Don't even begin to harbor the tiniest little bit of it. He could have bought this house for Maria. He might just have brought you here to look it over for him. To give a woman's opinion on furnishings and decor.*

But surely he couldn't be so cruel? Not even Nick at his most ruthlessly expedient would rub her nose in the failure of her unspoken aspirations this way.

She had to distance herself from him in order to preserve her feelings and her sanity. Trying to disengage her hand from his, she tugged away from him. Only to feel her fingers gently but irrevocably held.

"What's the matter?"

His voice seemed to dance across her nerve-ends, and she was afraid he'd feel her shuddering. As she stopped pulling, his thumb began to move slowly against her palm.

"What do you mean 'what's the matter'?"

She tried to bristle, but found it almost impossible. The hypnotic movement of his thumb was doing the strangest things to her heartbeat and her breathing.

But still she persisted.

"You kiss me off with a peck on the cheek and as good as disappear with Maria Rossi for six weeks...then suddenly materialize again and act as if nothing's happened!"

Nick released his grip, but in the beat of a heart, he held her again, one hand on each shoulder, fixing her in place as he looked down at her.

It was impossible to look away, and she didn't want to. The emotions in his extraordinary blue eyes were confused, shifting at astonishing speed between regret, guilt, determination...and others, more fiery yet less definable, ones that she hardly dare dream about, much less name.

"I'll explain everything to you, *cara mia.*" His voice was low, ragged in pitch, intent. "And I pray that you'll hear me out...and perhaps, if you think I deserve it, forgive me for hurting you."

"Who says you've hurt me?"

She forced herself to remain strong, not to succumb, even though every fiber of her being was urging her to melt, to fling herself forward, to taste those perfect lips. Why not grab what she could now in case there never was a chance again?

A frown puckered his broad brow. She wasn't fooling him at all. And yet when he took her hand again and drew her towards the broad, oak staircase with its solid no-nonsense banister, she still balked.

"Hey, not so fast!"

She dug her heels into the polished floor, halting him too. She did want what he wanted, yet it still seemed more foolhardy than flinging herself headlong off a cliff.

His frown deepened, but she saw sudden fear in his eyes too. Real fear.

"What is it, *cara?*"

"Look, this business of us sleeping together because it seems like a good idea at the time...and then deciding afterwards that it was a mistake. I've had enough of that. I...I—" She faltered, aware that she was revealing herself but overwhelmed by weariness at the thought of yet more dissembling with him. "I can't take it anymore, Nick. Not again."

"And you won't have to, *tesoro mio*," he said, no guile in his eyes.

Anna dragged in a breath, finally sensing that the complete truth was about to fall from his lips. For the first time. If she could take it.

"I didn't bring you here with the sole purpose of making love to you, Anna," he said, his face a picture of conflict that surely reflected her own. "But I can't deny..." His lashes swept down and up, so long and preternaturally dark in comparison to his lighter hair. "I can't deny that I want to."

"Then why upstairs?"

He shrugged.

"You'll notice if you look around, that there's no furniture to be seen. The only seating in the house is up there." He nodded towards the stairs, his strong shoulders lifting expressively.

The truth. The truth. Could she accept it? Bracing herself, she preceded him up the stairs. What if that truth meant that he was going to explain to her that he was planning to live here with—and marry—Maria Rossi?

Oh, but it was a lovely house. Even without the enhancement of furniture and art, Anna felt herself falling in love with the place. It was spacious, yet idiosyncratic, full of personality. She couldn't imagine an international film star, used to urban Italian chic, wanting to live here. But then she couldn't see a sophisticated cosmopolitan businessman like Nick here either.

And yet he was here. Courteously, he held open the door to a room that she deduced would look out on to the gardens that led down to the river, and let her enter.

She gasped. Not at the room, which was light and airy and inviting, but at the familiar piece of furniture that dominated it. One adorned with traditional dark carvings of fruits and vines...

"What's your bed doing here? I thought we were coming up here to sit on chairs?" she demanded, spinning around, her heart thudding.

What was he up to? The presence of his bed, the one from Villa Rosa where her life had changed forever, screamed of sex regardless of what he'd said.

"I thought it would make us feel more at home."

His eyes were on her as he loosened his fine silk tie and shrugged out of his dark suit jacket. In the absence of anywhere to hang it up, he folded it and placed it on top of a chest of drawers, the only other item of furniture in the room.

"Well, it's making *me* feel very nervous," Anna shot back, thoroughly confused. Seeing that bed made the prospect of ever resisting him recede even further, but she knew she had to know what was going on, where she stood.

"Look. If you want to talk, let's talk?" she rushed on, "Although I don't know what about. You made your thoughts on

203

this ridiculous relationship of ours pretty clear the last time we met."

"Well, basically, I wanted to talk about me being a complete fool."

Nick's voice was calm, wry and almost fatalistic. He strolled across to the bed and sat on the side of it, his long, dark-clad legs stretched out. "Please come and sit," he added softly, patting the duvet at his side.

Quite incapable of sorting out what she felt and what she wanted, Anna stayed where she was, just staring at him.

Nick measured out a good couple of feet on the surface of the coverlet. "Here—" he indicated, "—nowhere near me. I won't touch you or invade your space."

Fighting to appear composed, Anna moved forward and sat gingerly beside him.

"So talk," she said tightly. It was becoming very difficult to breathe. Especially as his cologne seemed to be seeping into her brain now, acting like an aphrodisiac and reminding her of other times when they'd been in close proximity, on this bed.

Nick looked down at his hands where they rested on his thighs. They were beautifully shaped, golden against the dark fabric of his trousers, but they were also tense, as if he were resisting some activity. Perhaps it was the urge to reach out?

A seemingly endless aching moment stretched between them. It seemed extraordinary that an articulate, accomplished man like Nick didn't seem to know what to say, where to start, but it did appear that he was lost for words. He'd always been such a smooth operator...

But finally, he said, "There's so much I have to explain. So much I want to elucidate and apologize to you for. But there's really only one thing I want to say first."

His eyes were like blue stars as he stared at her, and brilliant with such an expression of yearning that it almost stopped her heart. Despite his assurances of a moment ago, he reached for her hand and enclosed it in his own.

"*Ti amo*, Anna," he said simply, his gaze steady, open, inescapable, "I know you probably don't believe me. After what I've said and what I've done. But it *is* the truth. It has been for a long time. I just didn't recognize it."

The heart that had seemed to stop did a strange, slow, flip-flop inside her. She should tell him she didn't believe him—but she *did* believe him. He'd said it was the truth, but he hadn't needed to.

The truth was here, at last, in those beautiful blue eyes. Eyes that mirrored her own emotions, that reflected back the love she felt for him.

Suddenly, she didn't need the explanations and elucidations she knew he was about to offer. She would hear them in good time, but now her needs were different. She wanted just one thing. Well, more than one thing. She wanted to kiss him, to hold him, to be with him.

No questions. No strings. No doubts. No question of not trusting him.

She lifted their linked hands to her lips and pressed a kiss on the back of his.

"I believe you, Niccolo," she whispered against his hot skin, "And I love you." She looked at him, at his eyes again, recognizing a matching sense of wonder there.

"Anna."

The single word was ragged, intense, heartfelt, and the instant it left his lips they were in each other's arms, kissing, hugging, sighing and laughing as their hands roved hungrily over each other's bodies. It wasn't just a sensual exploration, but an affirmation. A renewed familiarization with all that was longed for and best loved.

As Anna began to tug at Nick's tie and his shirt, he halted her for a moment.

"Don't you want to—"

She stopped his hoarse, fevered words with the tip of her finger.

"Afterwards, *amore mio*," she whispered to him, feeling a surge of assured female confidence. Nick was the most alpha of alpha males, but for now *she* would choose. *She* would decide what happened when. Her love had empowered her.

With a soft laugh, and giving one of his extraordinary and toe-curlingly expressive and sexy shrugs, he threw himself wholeheartedly into helping her with the task of undressing him.

# Chapter Eleven

Later, much later, Anna lay watching the golden evening wane outside as she considered all the things he'd told her after they'd first made love.

It had been the most intense coming together yet. Passion had combined with ultimate tenderness, both of them gasping and sobbing with joy and relief, as happy to simply touch and hold each other and to lie with their bodies pressed together as they were to soar towards the pinnacle of pleasure.

Not that they hadn't soared, she reflected happily, aware of the foolish, Cheshire-cat grin that crept across her face, and the crimson blushes every time she relived the amazing chain of orgasms she'd experienced. That *they'd* experienced.

But afterwards, when they could both breathe again, the communion had been just as precious.

"I'll tell you about Maria now," Nick had begun, stoking her damp hair away from her brow.

Then he'd gone on to explain the circumstances of the Italian actress's car smash.

Anna's heart ached with sympathy for the beautiful but troubled woman who'd resorted to drink and drugs whilst worried about her career, the transitory quality of her beauty, and her confused, befuddled feelings about men and being loved by them. Maria had piled her Jaguar into a tree, under the influence, and then in the emergency room had asked frantically for Nick, the only man on her long list of former lovers whom she knew she could trust to help her and not reveal what had happened.

"She swore me to absolute secrecy," Nick had told Anna, gazing into her eyes as they lay facing each other, heads on the same pillow.

"Her career would be jeopardized if the circumstances of the crash got out—and she's been hurt before by exes spilling her secrets. I had to help her. Organize a discreet clinic, rehab and therapists, and yet tell nobody except the professionals involved."

Pain and regret darkened his eyes, but he didn't look away. "But I should have trusted you, *tesoro mio*." He reached out and touched her cheek. "You're the one I've always been able to trust. You never ratted on me when I was a wicked young man, sneaking out at night from Villa Rosa. Never once."

She pressed her hand to his, soothing the fingers that lay against her skin. "But you gave your word. And you kept it. I wouldn't expect anything less of you."

Nick's gaze was intense, amazed, but still shadowed.

"I'm a flawed man, *cara mia*," he sighed, "I've broken women's hearts...even though I never meant to. That was the last thing I ever meant to do to any woman. Least of all you." He paused, his long lashes flicking down for just a second, "And yet in the very act of trying to save you from me, I did it just the same. I've hurt you so much. Admit it. Haven't I?"

She drew in a long breath. This was the time for honesty.

"The situation between us has been...well...not so great. At times...yes."

She struggled for words, overwhelmed by the emotions she felt now, and those she had felt over the years, about this man.

"But I see now that you had your reasons. Things that your father said to me made me see that. They shed some light on the way you've acted. Or appeared to act."

Nick drew her closer to him, kissed her lips very softly, and then began to speak again.

"In the last few weeks I've spent more time talking with Carlo than ever before in my life. We've always both been busy, prickly with each other, unable to open up. But now, at last, I've learnt so much." He gave a small, fond smile, and Anna saw the great love there that he bore for his father, a man as strong, fiery and mercurial as he was himself.

"I always believed," he went on, "that he and my mother hated each other, and that their arguments were fuelled by resentment and suspicion and antagonism."

A fleeting expression of pure pain crossed his sculpted features and his mouth twisted. Anna laid her hand on his gleaming shoulder and he continued, "But I was young. I didn't understand how love could manifest itself in the most unlikely ways. That two people who absolutely adored each other could fall out like cat and dog, almost tear each other apart...yet still be the love of each other's lives." The pain transmuted, became wry humor, and Anna found herself smiling back at him, acknowledging a truth both universal and personal to the two of them.

"I always thought that I would be doomed in a relationship. Fated to destroy the life of any woman I loved and committed myself to. So I just refused to consider commitment."

His fingers moved on her face again, as if it were the most precious object in the world. "But now I see that was a coward's way of looking at life. A cop-out. My father and mother let their differences overwhelm their love and drive them apart." His blue eyes became incandescent, unblinking. "But I love you, Anna, and I'm going to fight for our relationship, *amore mio*. I'm going to be the man you deserve, and the man you need."

He paused, absolutely still and it felt to her as if the entire world were still around him. Waiting.

"If you still want me." A beat passed. His heart or her heart? Both in synchrony? "If you can love me?"

Coming back to the moment, still thinking of what Nick had said, Anna found tears on her cheek. Her heart felt as if it were about to burst with the love she felt for him, the love she'd expressed in feverish, whispered declarations, kissing his perfect face and molding herself against his hot, beautiful body. The confrontation of words had ignited, suddenly and with the sweetest of naturalness, into a less articulate but no less evocative manifestation of what she felt for him.

And now she was deliciously tired and sated and happy.

Oh, Niccolo Lisitano would never be an easy man to live with, but he was the one she wanted and loved and needed. In his own words, a life with Nick was worth fighting for, and she'd never been one to shrink from a challenge.

As her face once again cracked into the widest and most contented of smiles, she heard the pad of bare feet along the corridor outside, and then he was there in the doorway—the man she loved, and who she knew now loved her in return.

He was sublimely naked, smiling like a happy, mischievous schoolboy, and carried a bottle of champagne in one hand and a pair of slim crystal flutes in the other.

"To celebrate our engagement," he announced, flourishing the precious wine.

Anna sat up. "But we've been engaged six weeks, Nick," she said with a grin. "Not that I don't feel in the mood for bubbly, but isn't it a bit late?"

Nick set his booty down on the floor and slid onto the bed beside her. Anna felt her body clench deep in the quick of her at the sight of his golden magnificence so close, and at the arousing scent of his warm, primitive maleness. Oh yes, a glass of champagne would be lovely, but she could suddenly think of something far more delicious that made her mouth water.

His eyes grew serious, intent, as clear and honest and blue as an ocean.

"This is our real engagement, my love. Right here and right now," he said softly, reached for her hand, slid off the ring and then kissing the finger where it had been seconds before.

Kneeling up on the bed, naked and magnificent, he held the ring against her fingertip again and stared into her eyes.

"Anna Felgate, I love you. Will you do the honor of becoming my wife?"

"Yes. Oh yes!" she answered, every nerve, every cell in her body rejoicing and burning with love for him as the beautiful ring slid back home onto her finger. A second later, they were in each other's arms again, celebrating their engagement as a real union now, one that Anna knew would last far into the future and to the very end of their days.

It was quite some time before the bottle of champagne was finally opened.

# About the Author

Portia Da Costa is a multi-published British author of romance, erotic romance and erotic fiction. Her novels have been published by a variety of different houses, both in the US and the UK, and translated into many languages including German, Spanish, Italian, Dutch, Norwegian and Japanese. Portia has been writing for publication since 1990, and has had over twenty novels and 100 short stories published. She has contributed to many different short story anthologies and women's magazines. She lives in the heart of West Yorkshire, UK, with her husband and her cats. When she's not writing she can be found reading, watching TV and movies, hanging out on Twitter, and enjoying online life in general. She was formerly a librarian and has also worked in local government. To find out more about Portia visit portiadacosta.com/index.html, find her at her blog wendyportia.blogspot.com/ or follow her at twitter.com/PortiaDaCosta

*The first time they broke each other's hearts.*
*Now they have a second chance...*

# Breathe
## © *2010 Donna Alward*

Doing what was expected didn't get Anna Morelli anything but a bad marriage. Now that her life has fallen apart there's only one place she can think of to regroup and figure out what comes next. Two Willows, the winery owned by the only man she could ever rely on. Her oldest friend. And her worst mistake.

Growing up as the poor boy didn't stop Jace Willow from falling for Anna one hot, sultry summer. Back then, his best efforts to prove himself worthy of the Morelli standard fell just short. While it killed him to see her marry someone else, he made beating the Morellis at their own game his life's work. And he's excelled at it.

When Anna shows up on his doorstep, their painful history pales in the face of her need for a roof over her children's heads—and some peace. The heat of their renewed passion is healing, but it burns away layers of hard-won emotional distance, reopening old wounds. Threatening their one last chance to rebuild their love on the shattered pieces of their broken hearts...

*Warning: Full-bodied, rich bouquet with sexy overtones. Decant, breathe, and enjoy.*

*Available now in ebook and print from Samhain Publishing.*

*He'll let her have control...*
*until he's ready to make his move.*

# Pride and Passion
## © *2010 Jenna Bayley-Burke*

The only things Lily Harris inherits after her father's untimely death are debt, scandal and loneliness. She doesn't protest when her father's business partner, Jake Tolliver, steps up to help with the mess she finds herself in—until Jake reveals the last promise he made to her father.

Jake may be as compelling to look at as a marble statue—and stir a frighteningly powerful desire within her—but no way will Lily agree to be his socially acceptable bride while he continues to bed his string of beautiful women—not without getting him to agree to a deal of her own first.

With a well-earned reputation as a feral hunter who goes after what he wants, Jake has his sights set on Lily, and her lack of options puts her right where he's wanted her from the first moment he laid eyes on her.

Jake's not above making Lily think she's having it her way if that's what it'll take to have his way in the end. But once he grows tired of playing beast to her beauty, he's not above changing the rules of the game until they're both playing for the same prize.

*Warning: This title contains a hero used to getting what he wants, a heroine determined not to give in to him, some indecent proposals, a fair amount of pride, and enough passion to burn up everyone's control.*

*Available now in ebook and print from Samhain Publishing.*

# HOT STUFF

## Discover Samhain!

THE HOTTEST NEW PUBLISHER ON THE PLANET

Romance, fantasy, mystery, thriller, mainstream and more—Samhain has more selection, hotter authors, and everything's available in ebook.

Pick your favorite, sit back, and enjoy the ride! Hot stuff indeed.

SAMHAIN
PUBLISHING

WWW.SAMHAINPUBLISHING.COM

# GREAT
# CHEAP
# FUN

## Discover eBooks!

THE FASTEST WAY TO GET THE HOTTEST NAMES

Get your favorite authors on your favorite reader, long before they're
out in print! Ebooks from Samhain go wherever you go, and work with
whatever you carry—Palm, PDF, Mobi, Kindle, nook, and more.

SAMHAIN
PUBLISHING

WWW.SAMHAINPUBLISHING.COM

CPSIA information can be obtained at www.ICGtesting.com
Printed in the USA
BVOW070944191211

278720BV00002B/1/P

9 781609 284091